BLOOD PROSPECTOR

---★---

Calhoun swung the shotgun over to his left hand. He pulled a Dragoon with his right. He had a momentary concern that someone in the crowd might back shoot him as he turned toward Marks.

Then he saw that Mary had gotten up. She had grabbed her pistol and taken another from one of the bodies. She held one in each hand, facing the crowd.

Calhoun figured he was safe enough. She might not be able to withstand the crowd, but she could give him warning.

Marks had pushed himself up onto his hands and knees. He was shaking his head, trying to breathe.

Calhoun moved up and lifted his left boot and then stomped it down on the middle of Marks' back. Marks grunted and tried to rise again, but Calhoun held him face down.

"Should have learned some manners, sonny," Calhoun said with a sneer.

ALSO BY CLINT HAWKINS

**SADDLE TRAMP
THE CAPTIVE
GUNPOWDER TRAIL**

Published by
HarperPaperbacks

SADDLE TRAMP

GOLD AND LEAD

CLINT HAWKINS

HarperPaperbacks
A Division of HarperCollinsPublishers

This is a work of fiction. The characters, incidents, and dialogues are products of the author's imagination and are not to be construed as real. Any resemblance to actual events or persons, living or dead, is entirely coincidental.

HarperPaperbacks   *A Division of* HarperCollins*Publishers*
                   10 East 53rd Street, New York, N.Y. 10022

Cover illustration by John Thompson

First printing: January 1993

Printed in the United States of America

HarperPaperbacks and colophon are trademarks of HarperCollins*Publishers*

❖ 10 9 8 7 6 5 4 3 2 1

CHAPTER

* 1 *

The shovel bit deep into the rocky soil, but Wade Calhoun felt no satisfaction. While he enjoyed the well-oiled movement of his muscles under his faded cotton shirt, this job did not sit well with him. Not when he was standing here digging his own grave under the watchful eyes of eight hard-rock, pitiful miners.

Damn, he thought angrily, *if this don't beat all.*

Calhoun ached to kill these eight men. That thought lived as comfortably in his mind as a Plains Indian dwelled in his tipi. It wouldn't be easy, but he figured he could take care of near all of the men before they got him, even though most of them were sitting with guns in hand watching him.

The damn-fool miners had thought they had relieved Calhoun of all his weapons—making off with the two big Colt Walkers he carried in holsters on his saddle, as well as the Henry rifle and the double-bar-

reled shotgun. They had also gotten his twin-hol-
stered Colt Dragoons from around his waist as well
as the Bowie knife in the sheath that dangled like a
shoulder holster under his left arm. They now saw
him as a rattlesnake with its fangs pulled.

What they didn't know, though, was that Wade Calhoun always carried a cut-down version of a Walker in
a special small holster under his shirt at the small of
his back. A full-grown Walker was nearly five pounds
of .44-caliber pistol, with a nine-inch barrel. He had
taken one and cut the barrel down to about two inches, and he kept five of the six chambers loaded with
extra-heavy charges of powder. The hammer sat on
the sixth chamber, which was empty for safety's sake.
At close range, it was a devastating weapon.

It wasn't easy for Calhoun to refrain from calmly
stopping his work and taking off his shirt, when he
was too hot—which he was. He could do it in such a
way that by the time the shirt was off, the special
Walker would be in hand. He figured he could take
out five of these dim-witted miners right off. After
that, who knew what would happen.

But he kept his patience. It wasn't that he feared
dying. Indeed, he often seemed during the past several years to be courting it, seducing it as one would a
beautiful woman. Still, if he was going to die, he wanted to do it on his terms, if he could.

Besides, the miners seemed to be enjoying the
notion of this hard-eyed man digging his own grave.
Especially when Calhoun had the look of a gunman

about him. The miners might get lulled after a while, giving him a better opening. He could not see forcing things before they needed forcing. So he worked and sweated.

"You kin take a rest a minute, you want to," one of the miners said. "Wouldn't want ya to overdo yourself and be too tired for the hangin'." He guffawed, and the seven others joined him.

Calhoun jammed the shovel into the still-hard, rocky dirt in the hole and nodded. "I'd be obliged for a sip of water," he hinted.

The miner who had spoken before shrugged. He tossed Calhoun a canteen.

Calhoun nodded again. He opened the canteen and drank deeply. Then he pulled off his worn hat and poured a little water over his head, pleased with its freshening effect. "You mind was I to smoke?" he asked.

"Can't see why not," Willard Mossback said.

Calhoun capped the canteen and set it down. He reached into his shirt pocket and pulled out his cigarette fixings. Within moments he had expertly rolled and sealed one. He scratched a lucifer across his rough belt and then held the flame to the cigarette.

With the smoke billowing forth, Calhoun sat on the edge of the grave he had begun digging. Right now it was maybe six and a half feet long and two wide, but it was only a foot or so deep. He had a ways to go, he figured. Hoped might've been a better word. The longer he could keep digging, the more opportunity he would have to do something about his situation.

As he puffed, he thought back on how he had gotten into this predicament. As it had been so often in the past, these troubles could be linked to a horse. He never seemed to have any luck with horses. He either wound up with some sack of bones that not even the buzzards would deign to eat, or he got a good one that turned out to have no brains, or stamina or surefootedness.

The one that had brought these troubles on suffered from the latter. The big, tan horse was, for the most part, a good one, but he was as stumble-footed as a horse could be, always tripping over rocks, tree roots, even small sagebrush. It made for an annoying ride at times, especially up here in the mountains of Colorado Territory.

Calhoun was in no real hurry, since he had no place specific to go, or where he wanted to be, so he hadn't been riding all that hard. He had been just moseying along, minding his own business, when the horse stuck its left forefoot in a deep, narrow rut in what passed for a trail. With Calhoun's hundred seventy-five pounds on his back, plus the weight of weapons and supplies, the horse could not stop. The bone snapped audibly.

"Damn," Calhoun roared as he tumbled off the horse, frontward. The action added impetus to the animal's forward motion, ensuring that the foreleg broke, if there had been any doubt of it happening earlier.

The horse squealed and whinnied with pain and fright. Calhoun grunted and cursed as he landed almost head-first on the rocky ground. His right shoulder had taken the brunt of the fall, though he had managed to break some of it with his hands. He half rolled and came to a stop, sitting on a sharp rock, facing in the direction he had been going. The rock was uncomfortable, but the shoulder hurt like hell. He figured, though, even as he got up, that it was not broken.

Calhoun stood there rubbing his shoulder, looking at the horse for a moment. There was nothing that could be done for the animal now, except to end its misery. He thought of using his big Bowie knife, not wanting to waste powder and ball for the job. The horse was thrashing about too much, though, and Calhoun had more sense than to try to get too close to the horse's flying hooves.

"Dumb-ass horse," he muttered as he pulled one of his Dragoons. He calmly fired a ball into the animal's brain. It took some moments before the kicking stopped.

He finally moved in and struggled to free his saddle. It was his only really prized possession. It was handmade of fine, heavy leather. The Spanish-style saddle horn was huge. The skirts and Spanish-style stirrup covers had designs in silver worked by hand into the heavy leather. On each side of the saddle horn were the Walkers. On the right side was a saddle scabbard holding a Henry percussion rifle; and on the left was one encasing a double-barreled 10-gauge shotgun.

It took a while, but he finally got the saddle, saddle blanket, and saddlebags out from under the horse's weight. He set them aside, under a tree. He paused a few minutes to have a cigarette and rest a bit.

Then, with a look of distaste, he went and butchered out some of the meat from the horse. He hated horse-meat, but he was low on food, and it would do in a pinch. He dropped the meat in an old burlap sack. He looped the drawstring to the bag over his saddle horn.

Calhoun looked around. There was still plenty of daylight left, and he could see no reason for staying here any longer. He hung his saddlebags over his left shoulder. Then he hefted the big, heavy saddle sort of backhanded, so that his elbow stuck straight out forward, over the same shoulder.

With a sigh of resignation, he stepped off. He did not look forward to a long, tedious walk up this high in the mountains. He had no idea where the nearest town, or even mining camp, was. He knew that gold had been discovered here a year or so ago, setting off a new gold rush. Such things usually meant towns sprang up almost overnight. He hoped that was the case around here, since he would need to find a new horse. He also wouldn't mind a hot bath, a soft bed, and a willing woman.

The thought of those three things made the walking go a little easier, at least for a while.

He finally stopped for the night under the cover of some aspens and pines next to a sparkling rivulet of water maybe as wide as his hand. He gathered some wood and built a small fire. He plunked his butt on a rock and opened his small sack of supplies. He poured coffee into the pot he had filled from the rivulet, and put that on the fire to heat.

Then he sat for a few moments, contemplating his choices. They were limited, to be kind about it. He could gnaw on some hard buffalo jerky, or roast some of the horsemeat. Neither thrilled him. Finally he shrugged. It was summer, and even this high up it could get hotter than blazes. That meant fresh meat wouldn't last more than a day or two, at most. The jerky would last for weeks.

Calhoun cut a green stick maybe an inch around and three feet long. He sharpened one end and jabbed it through a hunk of horsemeat. Using rocks, he propped the stick up so the meat was dangling over the fire.

Calhoun scooped up a handful of water from the rivulet and splashed it in his mouth. He repeated the process several times, then tossed a couple of handfuls over his face.

While he waited for the meat and coffee to be ready, Calhoun rolled a cigarette and smoked it down. Then he ate, drank two cups of coffee, and smoked another cigarette. At last, he stretched out his bedroll, and slid inside it.

He had four more days of walking, before he saw another person. By that time, he was in poor humor. Not that he was ever in great humor, but this was even worse than usual.

He was soaked with sweat more often than not, and had been drenched by a sudden rainstorm that caught him in a meadow with no protection. By the time he reached the trees on the other side, the rain had stopped. The soles of his boots were wearing a little thin, his cotton shirt was threadbare, his hat ratty-looking, and his wool pants were in dire need of patching in several spots.

The only thing that had gone even vaguely well for him lately was hunting. He had been able to bring down something each day, whether it was a rabbit or a deer, or even a couple of squirrels once. Still, his other supplies were dwindling. He was getting a little low on powder and ball, and he was just about out of coffee and cigarette fixings.

It was getting late in the afternoon of his fourth day on foot when he heard something up ahead, and a little off to his right. He stopped and listened. It took only moments before he knew there was at least one horse out there. That worried—and excited—him a little. Utes prowled through these mountains, and they were warlike. He would hate to run into a war party of them that was too big to take on all by himself. That was only because he wanted to take as many Indians, of whatever kind he found, with him when he went.

He didn't much care which tribe they were from, really, though he held a special hatred of the Sioux. He figured they deserved it after what they had done to him and . . .

He heard a mule, and was suddenly certain that it

was a miner or group of miners out there, not Indians.

With something between relief and anger, he headed slowly toward the sound, trying to pick up more information with his senses before he got there.

Before he reached the small campsite, he had decided that it was one, at most two, men. He was not worried. As he neared it, down a small weed-covered path, he shouted, "Hello, the camp. Mind if I come by?"

He always felt like a fool calling out like that. However, he knew it was far better to do that and allay the fears of the person in the camp than to just walk in and risk being gut shot by some know-nothing tenderfoot or some damn-fool miner hoarding his precious hundred-dollar poke of gold.

"You alone?" a voice called.

"Yep."

"Come on ahead, then."

CHAPTER

* 2 *

Calhoun strolled into the camp. The tenor of the voice had told him that whoever was in the camp was nervous. Calhoun also figured the man had a gun out, hence Calhoun's easy entry. Calhoun's left hand was still holding up the saddle. His right hand dangled at his side, showing his peaceable intentions.

As Calhoun suspected, the man was a miner, and he was alone. He wore garb typical of his time and place—flannel shirt from out of which peeked the tops of red longjohns, Levi Strauss pants tucked into high-topped boots, and a battered slouch hat. The handle of a knife stuck up out of the top of one boot. The man held a Colt pistol in his right fist. He had no holster, and so Calhoun figured the man normally just tucked the revolver into his belt.

"Mind if I was to set a spell and take some coffee?"

"Nope." The man was not exactly garrulous. He

was short, thin, and reedy, but he appeared to be strong. He also had the fanatical look of gold fever about him. "Put your gear over there." He indicated a spot by a tree ten feet from the fire. "Leave your gun belt—and that big Bowie knife of yours—with the rest."

Calhoun's eyes tightened in anger. He was not the most peaceable man God ever made, and his temper was never very subdued. He brought himself under control with an effort. He turned and set the saddle and saddlebags down, grateful to be relieved of the burden, even if just for a short while. With some reluctance, he unbuckled the gun belt with his two Colt Dragoons and the dirk knife. He eased out the Bowie knife, knowing the miner was nervous and dropped it.

He turned and strolled nonchalantly to the fire, with his cup in his hand. He knelt and poured some coffee. He squatted, rocking back on his heels. After a sip of the terrible coffee, he said, "There's a couple rabbits in the burlap sack over with my gear."

The miner nodded. He had not put the pistol away. Still with it in hand, he backed toward Calhoun's gear. He did not take his eyes off the newcomer. He finally knelt and checked the bag, making sure it contained what Calhoun had said it had. He nodded and lifted the bag. As he walked back to the fire, he tossed the sack so that it landed in front of Calhoun.

"Cook 'um," he snapped.

It took several seconds for Calhoun to regain control of his temper, though his expression never changed.

"I said cook 'um," the miner growled. "And I meant tidday."

Calhoun sipped some coffee, then gently placed the cup down. "No," he said simply.

"Goddamn it to hell and back again seven times," the miner snapped. "You'll do what I say, or by Christ I'll drill a hole in you clear to next week."

"You'd get a heap more cooperation was you to treat folks better," Calhoun said quietly.

"Kiss my ass, bucko. I've seen the likes of you before. Too many goddamn times, too."

"What in the hell're you talkin' about?" Calhoun asked. He was beginning to think he had underestimated the man. The miner was giving off all the signs of gold-field paranoia.

"Shoot, as if you don't know. Bah." He spit into the fire. "Goddamn, you don't fool me for a second. Think you can come a-waltzin' in here, pretend to be some friendly cuss and then when my guard's down you and some cronies hidin' out in the bushes'll jump my ass, kill me, and make off with my poke."

"You're *loco,* mister," Calhoun said easily. He had been right in his assessment of the man's frame of mind. It didn't make the man deadly, but it sure as hell made him dangerous.

"No, I ain't," the man fairly screeched.

Calhoun shrugged and reached for the sack. "All right, so you ain't," he offered. "Lord, don't get your bowels in such an uproar." He pulled out the two rabbits, which he had gutted and skinned right after shooting them that afternoon. He would go along with this maniac for a while, until he got a chance to change his circumstances.

Still, it was galling that the man could be so raving that he couldn't see that Calhoun was alone and afoot. With a good look, anyone should be able to tell he had been on the trail for a while, without a horse. Finally he pushed those thoughts away. They were getting him nowhere, and there was nothing he could do to change the miner's mind right now.

He found two suitable sticks nearby and jammed them through the carcasses. He propped them over the fire.

"Some water over there," the miner said, pointing with his left hand toward a canteen. "You can wash up."

Calhoun nodded. As he cleaned the rabbit blood off his hands, he asked, "What's your name?"

"Whaddaya wanna know that fer?" the miner said.

Calhoun was amazed at the man's lunacy. "Just wonderin' is all. We're going to sup together, it might be nice to know who with."

"Who're you?"

"Wade Calhoun." Calhoun stood shaking water from his hands. He turned, wiping his hands on the front of his shirt. The hands gradually moved to the sides, and then around toward the back. Calhoun walked toward the fire, still wiping his hands, but at the same time surreptitiously pulled out the tail of his shirt. It would give him access to the cut-down Walker should he need it. He was certain now that he would, and soon.

"Harry Templeton," the miner said after a few moments. "Now set your thievin' ass back down over there before I plug ya."

Calhoun had had just about enough of this infuriating fool as he could stand. Still, he betrayed none of it as he squatted and took a few sips from his tin mug of coffee. Having sat around for a few minutes had done nothing to improve the flavor of the rancid brew.

Calhoun pulled out his fixings, making Templeton jump momentarily. The miner settled down some when he saw what Calhoun had brought forth. Calhoun rolled the smoke and started it with a burning twig from the fire. He held the cigarette in his left hand. Suddenly he slapped at his right thigh, then side.

Templeton, who had been smacking and scratching himself all along, grinned, sort of. "So you got the damn fleas, too, eh?"

"Don't everybody up this way?" Calhoun countered. "Damn infectious little critters." He knew full well that fleas were just one of the many hazards of this country. He paused. "What'n hell're you doin' out here by your lonesome?" he asked in even tones.

"I might ask the same thing," Templeton growled, tensing.

Calhoun shrugged. "Horse snapped its leg a few days ago. I been walkin' ever since."

"Oh?" Templeton didn't sound convinced. "And what'n the wide hell was you doin' out in these parts anyway?"

"Heard about the gold strikes last year. Thought I'd come out and see what it was all about."

"Bullshit. You ain't no goddamn miner, that's for goddamn sure."

"Ain't ever done it before," Calhoun said easily, continuing to swat at himself. "But every miner was somethin' before he was a miner."

"True enough," Templeton said. He still did not sound convinced.

Calhoun was sure Templeton was going to kill him—or try to. The only surprise was that he hadn't done so already. Calhoun reasoned that the man was not a cold-blooded killer and had to work himself up into a lather before he could pull the trigger. Calhoun judged that Templeton had just about convinced himself that Calhoun was a thief all set to make off with his poke.

Calhoun did not take kindly to being thought of in such a manner. Nor was he fond of having the fore-knowledge that the miner was going to blast him as soon as he worked up the nerve. Wade Calhoun also was the kind of man who never liked taking orders, especially when issued at the point of a gun and coming from a man who was a cranky, paranoid, trouble-making fool. He figured the time might have come for taking some action.

"Looks like those rabbits're about done," Calhoun

said. He looked up, squinting at Templeton, who had remained standing the whole time. "You aim to kill me before I've ate? Or are you gonna let me cross the divide on a full belly?"

Templeton was startled that Calhoun would know his thoughts.

"Now, was it me in your place," Calhoun went on conversationally, "I'd blast me here and now. That'd mean more food for you. It also would let you eat your supper in peace. You don't drop me before eatin', you'll have to set there the whole time keepin' an eye on me."

He shut up then, letting Templeton have time to let the thoughts fester in his brain briefly. Calhoun rolled and lighted another cigarette, watching the emotions play across Templeton's weather-browned, dull face.

Calhoun managed to keep the grin off his face when he saw the resolve build in Templeton's eyes. "Go 'head and do it, boy," Calhoun said softly, in a taunting tone. "Go 'head."

Templeton seemed almost in a daze. The pistol, once held loosely in his hand, was suddenly in a firm grip. Where moments ago it had been pointed downward at the ground in Calhoun's general direction, it now bore down on Calhoun's chest.

Calhoun suddenly did three things at the same time. He flipped his cigarette at Templeton's face, stood, and reached around back with his right hand to yank out the cut-down Walker.

Once again Calhoun managed to keep from grinning when he saw the look of shocked surprise on Templeton's face. It wasn't so much that Calhoun was pleased that he was about to kill this idiot; it was that he had been able to win out despite this other man having the drop on him for twenty minutes. That, and the fact that he had deduced it in enough time to prevent his death.

Templeton was still raising his pistol, trying to increase his speed, but his own actions seemed to be happening in slow motion. Calhoun's on the other hand were moving at the speed of a rushing river.

Calhoun fired twice. The blast from the short-barreled revolver with the extra-heavy loads of powder was tremendous. Both lead balls punched all the way through Harry Templeton, knocking the miner sideways and down.

Templeton lay on the ground, realizing that his life was flowing rapidly out of him. He realized he had been foolish, and should have shot his visitor straight out. Despite his months in the mountains though, he was still a little too civilized for such a thing. Most of the men who spent much time around the mining camps often lost all vestiges of civilization. Some didn't.

Templeton tried to raise up. He wanted to get off at least one shot, but none of his systems were working. It seemed like everything that connected his body parts had gone awry. He finally sighed and gave up the fight, just as he saw Calhoun looming over him.

"Pitiable fool," Calhoun muttered as he knelt and gently pulled the Colt from Templeton's almost lifeless fingers. He pitched the pistol into the woods.

He rose, shaking his head at the wastefulness of it all. It was, he thought, incredibly harebrained that someone could be so caught up in his lust for gold that he got himself killed for nothing. It was one thing to go under while defending your family or something. That was Calhoun's main regret, that he was not there to defend his family, to take out some of the enemy when the Sioux had . . .

"Damn," he mumbled in anger. He had been in a poor mood before, and it had soured further. It wasn't bad enough that Harry Templeton had goaded him into this killing, but the episode had also brought back the demons of Calhoun's past. Calhoun didn't like that.

With a scowl, he turned and went to his gear. He buckled on his gun belt, and stuffed the Bowie into the sheath under his arm. Then he returned and squatted by the fire. He pulled one of the rabbits toward him, sliced off a chunk with his dirk and stuffed the meat in his mouth. He sat, eating silently, without much enthusiasm, his back toward the corpse.

He finally finished eating, and then had another cup of coffee with a cigarette. He rose and turned, looking down at Templeton's body. He was half tempted to leave the thing for the wolves and coyotes and whatever other scavengers happened along.

Then he sighed. Templeton had suffered enough by being a damn fool and getting himself killed far too young. He deserved at least the dignity of a burial.

Calhoun found a shovel among Templeton's belongings. Off to the side of the little campsite, he found a place that seemed soft enough to dig. Reluctantly, he jabbed the shovel in. With growing irritation, he sent the dirt flying in all directions, his anger sending bursts of energy through him.

It was dark when he finally finished digging. He dragged the corpse over to the hole and rolled it in. He tossed an old blanket in atop it before starting to pitch dirt in. By the time he finished the onerous task, he was in a black mood. Still, he had started the job, and he'd be damned if he'd let it go halfway. He gathered a few rocks and piled them on the new grave.

He cleaned and reloaded his stubby Walker. Then he hung the other cooked rabbit in a tree and turned in.

He awoke still in a foul mood, but as he polished off his first cup of coffee, he realized things weren't so bad after all. He had more than two hundred dollars on him, which was far more than he generally had. Templeton's horse and a mule were nearby and both seemed healthy. He could ride and have a pack animal. Seeing as how Templeton had left a heap of supplies, too, the latter would be a good thing.

He ate the second rabbit, downed more coffee, and smoked a cigarette. Then he proceeded to pick

through Templeton's supplies. He had no use for the
usual miner's equipment he found, so he tossed it
aside. Still, there was food, coffee, canned goods,
powder, lead, cigarette fixings, a few pots and pans,
and a leather bag with what Calhoun estimated was
six hundred dollars' worth of gold in it.

CHAPTER

* 3 *

Calhoun stood for some minutes, holding the bag. It was more money than he had ever held in his hand at one time. The thought of what he could do with such a small fortune was intriguing.

Then he half grinned. He had no use for that much money, really. He knew full well that he'd end up blowing all the gold on seeing the elephant in some fancy town somewhere. He would, he admitted silently, have a hell of a spree, but the money would do little to better his life. It would not bring back Lizbeth and Lottie.

"Damn," he growled. He more than half wished that he had found the money last night and buried it with Templeton. He decided that whenever he got to the nearest town, he would see if anyone knew if Harry Templeton had any kin. He would just tell them he had some of the man's effects and wanted to forward them. Lord knew, he couldn't mention the fact that the poor fellow had had six hundred dollars' worth of gold on him. That would bring a stampede of "relatives."

Calhoun began packing the mule, making sure the bag of gold was well secured—and buried under a lot of innocuous food items. There was too much chance of an encounter with a band of outlaws on the trail, men who would have no compunction about killing for a dollar, let alone six hundred.

Within an hour, he was riding out on Templeton's well-behaved reddish roan. The mule trailed complacently along behind.

Two days later, he was still moseying along, when he heard the telltale sounds of a mining camp. It wasn't a town, exactly, but it would have to do for now. The men here might know Templeton. They might also know where the next real town was.

He rode into the squalid camp. A painted sign nailed to a tree said it was called Misfortune. Tents stuck up wherever there was a clear space. Old wood, garbage, equipment, empty kegs, and assorted other trash was strewn all about. The stench was overpowering, since the men had made no arrangements for handling their wastes.

The St. Louis River poured down from a cleft in the rocks to the west and bubbled toward the center of the camp. As it wound through Misfortune though, it widened and even pooled in spots. It still had a strong current, but it was not very deep. At its widest near the camp, it was perhaps fifty feet across.

Men either knelt on the shore or stood in the freezing water to work their pans or rockers. A man shouted something, then pointed straight at Calhoun.

The others stopped their work to turn and stare, as Calhoun let the roan pick its way down the rocky hill toward the sunken camp. Calhoun was surprised to see two women come out of tents. Even at the distance, he was fairly certain they were not fallen angels. Most likely wives of a couple of the men. That was odd, but not unheard of in such places.

The men gathered in a sort of rugged semicircle. Calhoun stopped the horse. A big, hard-looking man was in the center. Calhoun pegged the man for the leader of this raggedy bunch of tin-pan miners. He was a big, broad-shouldered man with a no-nonsense look about him. While his face held no cruelty, it did not hold much compassion, either. He wore dark Levi's tucked into tall black boots and the top of his longjohns served as a shirt. Suspenders dangled down from his waist.

"Whatcha doin' wit' that hoss, mister?" the big man asked.

"Ridin' him," Calhoun said evenly. His hackles were already raised. He sat with hands crossed on the saddle in front of him, near enough to let him get at the Dragoons quickly but not so near as to make the miners nervous.

"That ain't what I meant, goddamn it," the big man snarled.

"It's what you asked."

The big man spit. "Where'd ya get the hoss? And the mule?"

"Back up the trail a couple days."

"They just wanderin' 'round loose?"

"Might've been. Who wants to know?"

"Name's Chris Winslow." His voice and face grew hard. "Now, boy, where'd you get them goddamn animals?"

Calhoun wondered just how much he should tell these men. In such a place, these men would be their own law. Whatever they did would be accepted by anyone else who heard about it—*if* anyone else ever heard of it. Still, lying often brought more trouble than it avoided.

"Got 'em from Harry Templeton, about two days back."

"He just give 'em to you?" Winslow asked. He looked tough and competent, and a no-nonsense man to boot.

"Not exactly," Calhoun said wryly.

Winslow spit again. "You got about one goddamn minute to tell us what happened, or we'll string your scrawny neck from a tree."

"Scrawny?" Calhoun asked. Wade Calhoun was a couple inches short of six feet tall and weighed in the neighborhood of one seventy-five. His face, pocked from a childhood case of acne, was hard and mean looking. He certainly could not be seen as scrawny.

"Will be once the rope's done with ya. Your time's runnin' out, boy."

Calhoun rubbed a hand across the lower half of his face for a moment. He used the time to take in the knot of men facing him. They were a rough-looking bunch, men hardened by living in harsh mining camps, fighting off claim jumpers and other miscreants, wading in freezing rivers for a handful of gold.

Calhoun's first inclination was to yank out his Dragoons and just start blasting. Such things did not set well with him, though. At least not without reason. He had seen no compelling reason for it now. Besides, he more than half admired these men. They broke their backs, facing all sorts of priva-tions, troubles, and dangers to follow a dream. He had had a dream once, but it had been shattered. Never again had he had another, nor did he think he ever would.

Still, the life of these tin-pan miners almost invari-ably led them to harden themselves against all oth-ers, to become suspicious of everyone, paranoid that everyone was out to jump their claim or steal their pitiful stash of gold. Just as Templeton had been.

"I shot him," Calhoun finally said.

Winslow's eyes widened in surprise. He wasn't shocked so much that Templeton had gotten himself killed, but rather that the man on Templeton's horse so readily admitted doing it. "What's your name, boy?" Winslow asked.

"Wade Calhoun."

"You mind explainin' why you killed poor Mister Templeton?" He paused a fraction of a second. "To our court."

"I would mind," Calhoun said, tensing for action. Then he heard the distinctive snicking of two hammers being cocked.

"Mister Armitage behind you ain't got the best eyesight in God's creation, but with that scattergun he's holdin', it won't make a hell of a lot of difference," Winslow said calmly. "Now, you can come peaceably. Or in pieces." He chuckled at his little joke.

The others stayed stone-faced, finding no humor in the death of one of their own.

Calhoun shrugged. He had no choice. He would have to wait and see what developed. He knew, though, that he had no chance at all of being allowed to leave here. These men would try him on whatever charge they conjured up, and sentence him to hang. It was the way of things, and he acknowledged it. That didn't mean he had to accept it, though.

Two men hauled him off the horse and stripped him of his weapons. The action was not as gentle as it could have been. As the two, helped by a third and followed by the shotgun-toting Mr. Armitage, hauled him toward one of the tents, he noticed two other men going through the supplies on the pack mule.

Within half an hour, the court, such as it was, was

convened, with Winslow acting as judge, as well as prosecutor. Calhoun had no defense, other than when he managed to get a word in here and there. Since the outcome was a foregone conclusion, the rest was just a formality. Calhoun had seen it before, and it always annoyed him. These men were about to commit murder, had made up their minds to do so, yet they insisted on this charade so they could give themselves airs about justice done.

It was over swiftly, and surely, with the pronouncement that Calhoun would be hanged by the neck until he was dead. The hanging would take place before dark.

"Jus' one thing before we end this here proceedin'," Winslow said pompously. "What'd you do with poor Templeton's body. We'll need to see the remains're brought back here."

"Buried him," Calhoun said calmly. These men had tried to goad him into admitting something all along, but he had not lost his outward serenity, through it all. He had admitted killing Templeton, that was enough for the miners. They were not interested in really hearing circumstances, though they tried to salve their consciences by getting him to admit that it was cold-blooded murder.

"Buried . . . him . . . ?" Winslow seemed dumbstruck.

"Yep. Hole in the ground and all. Rocks on top so the animals couldn't get at him." Calhoun suddenly felt good about all the effort he had put into that burial. It might not do him any good in this world, but perhaps it would benefit him in the next.

Winslow shook his head. "I reckon I don't believe you, Mister Calhoun," he finally said. "It's just a story you concocted to make us have some pity on your miserable hide."

"I don't much give a shit what you believe," Calhoun snapped, letting just a bit of his anger surface. "You ain't believed a damn thing I've said since I got here—except when I said I shot down Templeton." He paused. "It's true, though. Just 'cause I shot him didn't mean I hated him. I was just tryin' to keep my own ass from gettin' shot."

He clamped his lips shut. He was not used to giving such long-winded speeches, and it always embarrassed him on those rare occasions when it happened.

"Where'd you do it?" Winslow asked. He still did not believe Calhoun, but he was beginning to doubt his own certainty.

"Just some spot he was camped. It was almost two days' ride south of here. I can take you there, if you're of a mind to see it, maybe pay your last respects." He almost sneered.

"Oh, we'll be checkin' on it, boy," Winslow said. He was angry that he was doubting his own resolve. "But you ain't gonna be 'round to lead us there. You got a date with the hangman—me. And I ain't of a mind to wait any longer. Let's get it done."

He raised the butt of his revolver to gavel the trial to a close. He stopped with the pistol in midair when one of the miners shouted, "Wait!"

"You got somethin' to say, Hugh?" Winslow asked, annoyed at the interruption.

"Sure do." Hugh Stampp was short and round, but not much of it looked like weak fat. He had been Harry Templeton's best friend in Misfortune, and was sad to hear of his demise. He was glad, though, that they had caught the culprit, who was about to pay the ultimate price. Still, Stampp had an idea.

"Well, speak up, damn it," Winslow snapped. "We got business to tend to so's we can get back to our pannin'."

Despite his sense of loss, Stampp smiled. "Well, I was just thinking here," Stampp said with precise diction, "that since this killer here likes to dig graves so much, maybe he ought to dig his own."

Winslow's eyes widened in interest. He gently placed the pistol down, acknowledging that this trial was not quite over just yet. "How do some of you other boys feel about that?" he asked.

"Hell with it," one shouted. "Let's just hang the son of a bitch and be done with it. There's gold waitin' out there in that water."

"Anybody else?" Winslow asked.

"I like Hugh's idea," Armitage said.

He was an unusual man to be in such a place. The miners, especially placer miners like these, were almost invariably young men. It took a young man to handle the demands of such work. Leo Armitage, with his nearly bald head, white beard, and brass-rimmed spectacles, looked out of place in this setting. Still, he had carried his load of work, and the men valued his input, since he was far more educated than any of the others.

"Why?" the one who had spoken out against it said. He sounded angry. To Ian Dougherty, any minute away from his gold panning was a minute wasted in his quest for wealth. It made no matter that he had been out here nearly a year and hadn't made a total of two hundred dollars. He just knew he was going to hit the mother lode of panning one day.

"Because," Armitage said, "I work hard enough all day out there in the river. I don't need to add to my burden by digging a grave for some murderer. Is there any one of you who would *like* to do some extra work?"

He got no answer, since the answer was obvious.

Still, Dougherty was unsatisfied. "Hell, just pitch his dead ass in the river. Or drag him out in the woods. Let the goddamn animals have him. They got to eat, too."

"We ain't savages," Winslow snapped. "Man should have a Christian burial." He felt full of God's grace at the moment.

"Besides," Stampp interjected, "it'll give him time to think about what evil he committed. All the while he's there digging that hole, he'll be thinking of what brought him to it."

"It'd sure as hell break the goddamn monotony 'round here, too," another man added. "Give us a little goddamn entertainment while we watch that murderin' son of a bitch diggin' his own hole."

The men had a chuckle about it, before Winslow rapped for attention. "All right, boys," he finally said, "anybody but Ian here dislike the idea?"

No one did. "Sorry, Ian," Winslow said. He didn't look it. "You've been outvoted. Let's get it done." He slammed the pistol butt on the table with finality.

CHAPTER
* 4 *

S o now Calhoun sat here on the rim of his own shallow grave, puffing on a cigarette. He took another sip of water, appreciating its coolness after the hard labor. He capped the canteen again, and tossed it toward Willard Mossback, the miner who had given him the canteen in the first place.

Mossback caught the canteen and grinned. He was enjoying this little diversion.

Calhoun bent over and jammed his cigarette butt into the crumbling dirt between his boots. He froze there, staring down. Slowly he reached out and grabbed a handful of the soil and rolled it around in his fingers a moment.

"Best get your ass back to work, son," Leo Armitage said roughly. "Unless you want a shallow grave for your eternal resting place."

Calhoun ignored him, still, crumbling the dirt in his fingers. Finally he felt a spot of rough hardness.

Still with the one hand, he sifted the soil, until he held only the hard little nugget.

"Come on, damnit," Ian Dougherty snapped. "Hustle your ass. We got us work to do."

"Maybe you'll be interested in this," Calhoun said, rising. He tossed the nugget to Dougherty.

It hit Dougherty in the chest. He bent and picked it up. "Goddamn!" he yelled excitedly. "A goddamn nugget!"

Several men crowded around Dougherty to look, excitement brightening their otherwise drab faces.

Big Chris Winslow waved a hand, and two men—a bull-necked idiot named Enos Pennrose and the plump, but hard Hugh Stampp—jumped into the grave. They grabbed Calhoun under the arms and lifted him out. With a good shove, they sent him sprawling out of the way.

Winslow hopped into the slight excavation and pushed his two friends roughly aside. He knelt where the small butt of Calhoun's old cigarette stuck out of the soil. He combed his fingers through the soil, snagging on rocks. The effort produced another small nugget.

The other miners began to gather around, excitement building, as Winslow raked his hands through the dirt again.

Calhoun almost smiled. He quietly pushed himself up and brushed himself off. His movements were slow and deliberate, designed not to attract attention. Slowly, calmly, he began backing toward the trees ten yards behind him. He made it within a few moments. He whirled and ducked into the cover of the trees.

Without haste, but without delay, he worked his way toward one of the tents. He had seen the miners carrying his equipment and supplies in there as he had been dragged off before his "trial." All his things were there, having been pitched recklessly inside the tent.

As he buckled on his gun belt and hung the sheathed Bowie knife around his neck, he felt something akin to relief. Excitement, too. There was a passel of thieving, murderous punks out there, men who had tried to kill him for no good reason. They were about to get their comeuppance.

"Hey!" he heard someone outside shout. "Where the hell's the murderin' son of a bitch gotten to?"

"Find him!" Winslow's voice was distinctive.

Calhoun quickly checked the loads in his pistols. Then he stepped outside of the tent, one Dragoon in his right fist. "You boys lookin' for me?" he yelled.

The miners stopped in their frantic, useless search, and looked toward the voice. Without hesitation or compassion, Calhoun blasted the miner nearest him. He had never learned the man's name.

The miner doubled over and then fell onto his face, clutching his stomach. Calhoun knew the man was alive, but he also knew that with the intense pain brought by a .44-caliber bullet in the guts, he would be capable of doing nothing.

Calhoun snapped the Dragoon up and fired again.

That ball caught Winslow in the shoulder, spinning him half to the side. Calhoun fired again. The bullet pierced Winslow's side, cracking ribs and ravaging the big miner's heart and lungs.

Winslow fell, hard, landing with the side of his face up on the ground just outside the grave.

A shot whistled through the left sleeve of Calhoun's shirt. He spun, crouching, and snapped off another shot.

Hugh Stampp's body jerked with the impact of a bullet. He looked like he was about to say something, but he made no sound other than a whispery moan and melted to his knees. His pistol dropped on the ground, forgotten, as Stampp looked at the blood streaming from the big hole in his chest.

Calhoun rose from his fighting crouch. The miners had, for the most part, turned tail and run, seeking the shelter of the woods. Calhoun caught a glimpse of Ian Dougherty creeping around the corner of a tattered cabin tent. The shelter was nearest the St. Louis River, which ran roughly west to east here.

Calhoun swung that way. "Come on and drag your ragged ass out here, Dougherty," he snapped.

Dougherty hesitated, but then moved away from the tent, coming toward Calhoun. He stopped fifty feet from Calhoun, the pistol in his hand dangling alongside his left leg.

Calhoun slid the Dragoon away. It had only one more shot in it, and he wanted to have more firepower available, if it was needed. He eased out the other Dragoon, and held it downward. "Well?" he asked, shouting to make sure he was heard across the abyss of emptiness.

"Well what?" Dougherty called back. His voice was nervous.

"You was so all-fired anxious to kill me a while back."

"Those other fools'd listened to me, they'd all be alive now."

"Reckon that's so." Calhoun paused. "I was wonderin' if you was still anxious to see me dead."

"I am." Dougherty's voice had gained a little in firmness.

"Looks like you're on your own for it, boy."

"I know." The nervousness had crept back into Dougherty's voice.

"Then shit or get off the pot, Dougherty. I got other business and no time to stand here passin' the time of day with the likes of you."

Dougherty hesitated. Without the support of seven armed friends, he was no hero. Indeed, he was no hero at the best of times. That was why he wanted Calhoun to be hanged straight off. To a man of his limited bravery, such a thing was expeditious. It hadn't happened, and now he was standing here face to face with this flinty-eyed gunman.

Dougherty had thought when he first started going around the tent that he might be able to bushwhack Calhoun. Then he saw Calhoun shoot down Winslow and Stampp without so much as breaking a sweat. It was then that Dougherty knew he was in too deeply. Still, there was no easy way for him to back out of it now. He had to press ahead.

He started raising the pistol slowly, knowing that his hand was trembling a little. As his arm moved, though, he seemed to gain confidence. Or maybe it was just fear goading him. The arm speeded up, moving rapidly upward.

Dougherty could not believe it. Calhoun still had not moved. A wave of euphoria swept through Dougherty. He had a chance now. *I fooled you, Calhoun, goddamn it!* he thought. The damn fool of a gunman had underestimated him; he had even fooled himself a little with the speed at which he was moving.

It came as a severe shock to Dougherty, then, when a ball from Calhoun's Dragoon punctured his left lung. A numbness spread from the wound, radiating outward. He was surprised there was so little pain. It felt like he had been punched a good blow to the chest. He had taken such things before and weathered them easily.

With that knowledge, he figured he could still get a shot off and take Calhoun down for sure. The thought gave him confidence.

Trouble was, he soon found out his confidence exceeded his abilities. Learning that stunned him as much as taking the bullet had. It was particularly annoying, too. He had always been strong, and he could not understand why he could not even lift his arm. He also wondered why the ground seemed to be rising up to meet him.

Calhoun stood there with a smoking Dragoon in hand, watching for the two seconds it took Dougherty to fall. Once the miner was down, Calhoun lowered his Colt pistol. He turned slowly, senses alert. It would be just like one of these miners, he thought, to hide behind a tree and shoot him in the back. He neither saw nor heard anything out of the ordinary.

He slid the pistol away and walked back to the tent where his gear was stored. There he swiftly reloaded both Dragoons. Then he checked his weapons on the saddle before dragging the saddle outside. He found his horse tethered to a tree nearby.

As he began saddling the animal, he noticed both women from the camp watching him from their own tents. He wondered again about them. One was old—or maybe she just looked old. The other, from what Calhoun had seen of her at a distance, was rather attractive. He did not know their names, nor to whom they were attached. He shrugged and finished his job.

Afterward, he went back in the tent and gathered up what supplies he had had before. He loaded them on the mule again. He thought he had everything and was almost ready to mount the reddish roan, until he thought about the bag of gold. It was not with the other supplies.

He meandered through the camp, almost arrogantly, entering one tent after another, looking around for the leather sack. He avoided the two tents where the women were, though they were among the closest. In the last one he tried on his side of the river, he found the sack.

Calhoun casually strolled back to the animals, and looped the drawstring of the gold sack over the mule's pack saddle.

He climbed onto his roan and rode off, along the trail on which he had arrived. As he passed near the tents where the women were, he tipped his hat in false civility. The two women still stood in the openings of the tents, watching silently.

A closer look had confirmed what he had thought about the women. One was older and seemed worn out by a hard life. The other was fairly young and attractive, though she also looked like life had not treated her all that well. He supposed that with her good looks, and considering the pecking order he had seen in the camp, she must be the wife—or at least the woman—of Chris Winslow.

Not that any of it mattered. The women meant nothing to him, though he did consider for just a moment asking them if they wanted to go with him, if only to be rid of the place. He decided, though, that he would be in a pickle if they chose that course. He did not need nor want any companionship. Not even that of an attractive young woman, if that meant all the troubles they would bring.

Not long after, he came to a crossing of the trails. He turned northwest, that being a direction that seemed as good as any other to him right now. He had no place to be, and nowhere to go. He did, however, have more money than he ever thought he would have at one time. With the two hundred twenty-seven dollars of his own money, plus the estimated six hundred dollars in gold, he could have himself a hell of a spree in whatever town he came across.

He had no regrets about having taken the gold. He had originally wanted to turn it over to someone who could prove he was related to Harry Templeton. However, the actions of the miners back in that wretched little camp had quickly dispelled him of that notion. Calhoun figured that he was due the money, considering the miners' treatment of him. It was, after all, only right out here in these wild lands.

He pushed on past dark, letting the horse pick its slow way along the dark trail. While Calhoun did not fear the miners, they were hard men, and might well consider coming after him. Calhoun figured there was no reason to put himself in danger when such a thing was uncalled for.

Along about midnight, he figured he had put enough distance between himself and the mining camp. He pulled off the trail and tied the horse and mule. He did not bother to unsaddle the former or unload the latter. He simply gnawed down a couple pieces of jerky, swallowed a few mouthfuls of water, and then turned in.

He was more surly than usual the next morning. Still, he felt a little regret at having neglected the animals. He was not the type of man who took a horse to heart. Not with the way his luck ran with those critters. He considered them as tools, or equipment. As such, though, they deserved decent treatment if they were to be expected to perform properly.

He had taken some grain in a sack from the mining camp. He put feedbags full of grain over each beast's head and let them eat their fill. Afterward, he allowed them to drink from the seeping spring he found nearby.

He also took the time to cook himself a decent meal, since he was as hungry as a bear. Finally, he pulled himself into the saddle and rode off. His spirits were somewhat improved, and he was feeling a bit of urgency. He decided that he needed to get to a town and blow off some steam as soon as possible.

CHAPTER

✱ 5 ✱

Towns, however, were few and far between out here in these imposing, purplish mountains. Two days after leaving the mining camp, he had spotted no sign of a town of any kind, and his spirits flagged. Calhoun was irritated with life in general, and these empty Rocky Mountains in particular.

Wade Calhoun was not a man who desired company often or for long periods of time. But there were occasions when he wanted some companionship. Usually it was that of a woman, but every once in a while, he would settle for the rough pseudo-camaraderie of a saloon full of boisterous men and the excitement of a poker game.

Calhoun awoke feeling groggy. He usually snapped awake alertly, especially in the dark like this, when something alerted his subconscious. He was irritated that he had not done so this time.

Still, his instincts were working, which was better than nothing. Something had woken him; something faint had filtered into the deep inner recesses of his mind. His instincts and training had taken over from there.

Though he had come awake, he had not moved, other than to make sure his right hand had a tight grip on one of the Dragoons. Then he waited, trying to pick out sounds.

He heard it again. He didn't know what it was that had caused it, but he knew now where it was coming from—where he had stacked his supplies. It did not sound like a bear or wolf or other animal, and since the noise was coming from the supplies, he assumed it was a person.

Who could be out here, though? he wondered. There was nothing around here that he knew of, except the aptly named mining camp of Misfortune a couple of days' ride away.

He decided it didn't matter. Whoever was here was rummaging through his supplies. He had had quite enough trouble in the past week or so, and his temper was short. He was not about to let some down-and-out tin pan rifle his supplies.

Soundlessly, Calhoun slid out of his bedroll, feeling the coolness of the air. It was just before dawn, and the blackness was broken only by the sliver of a moon far off and the thick layer of stars overhead.

He slid the Dragoon into the hard leather holster. In stocking feet, he crept toward his supplies, skirting the small pile of embers that had been his dinner fire.

Calhoun saw the furtive movement of a shadow, and he charged. Suddenly he jumped. He hit the figure somewhere around the lower ribs of the back on one side. His strong arms encircled the figure as his momentum carried them into a roll through the dirt, leaves, and brush.

The two came to a stop with Calhoun half on top of the still-unseen enemy. He jerked his right fist back to around his ear, cocked and ready to launch it. To keep his target steady, Calhoun slapped his left palm down on his foe's chest. The move left him shocked.

He froze where he was, right hand still cocked, left on the heaving bosom of a woman. "Damn," he breathed, wondering just what in hell he had gotten himself into this time.

He dropped his right hand, releasing the fist at the same time. As he stood, he wrapped his left hand into a fist that encircled a handful of cloth. He dragged the woman up with him.

"I don't know who the hell you are, or what the hell you're doin' out here," Calhoun snapped, "but I'll shoot you dead the first sign of trouble you give me."

He got no response, annoying him all the more. Everything bothered him these days, and that fact only added to it all. He jerked the woman forward and then shoved off as he spun, so that she was ahead of him, facing the old fire.

He pushed her back when she did not move. That got her going. She stopped at the little ring of stone encircling the soft orange glow of the embers. "Sit," he ordered.

The woman did nothing, so Calhoun shoved down hard on her shoulder. The woman's knees buckled and she sank down. With her sitting, Calhoun marched around to the other side of the fire, where he could keep an eye on the woman. He tossed some wood on the fire and waved his hat. The embers glowed hotly, and then small fingers of flame leaped up, licking at the twigs. Calhoun added some larger pieces of wood. All the while, he watched the woman peripherally.

With the fire burning brightly, he sat back and really looked at the woman for the first time. He managed to keep from showing his surprise—and rage. Her round, dark Indian face stared passively back at him.

All the hatred that the Sioux had aroused in him some years ago flooded back into him, and it was all he could do to keep himself from yanking out a Dragoon and blasting this heathen squaw into eternity.

It helped that she was quite pleasantly featured. He had to admit that, though he did not want to. He also did not want to admit that her attractiveness was marred by the bruises on her face, once he had seen them. With her dark skin, the dim light and the odd shadows thrown by the fire, the marks had been hard to see.

He supposed she had the marks of beatings elsewhere, too. She might be an Indian, but Calhoun hated to see any woman abused in such a way.

Still, he was a little concerned now. It was not likely that an Indian woman would be wandering around these mountains alone. That meant there was a good chance of warriors lurking about. He was not afraid of them, but he did not want a bunch of skulking warriors coming at him from behind trees. He much preferred to face them out in the open.

"You speak English?" Calhoun finally asked, pushing the worrisome thoughts out of his mind.

He got no response, which did little to improve his outlook about either life or this woman. He was about to bellow at her, threaten her, whatever it took to get her to talk.

He stopped himself before anything came out, though. It was evident she had been treated roughly already. She had lived through that, and, being an Indian, probably had done so stoically. She would do the same with him, he reasoned.

With a sigh to try to settle himself, Calhoun picked up his coffee mug and filled it from the pot that had been left to keep warm all night. He reached around the fire with the cup, holding it out for the woman.

She tried to hide the surprise she felt, but it sparkled in her dark eyes for just a moment. Then she looked straight ahead.

"I ain't gonna poison you," Calhoun said quietly. "Go on and take it."

She still made no effort to take the cup. Calhoun nodded, still battling his anger. He set the cup down as near to her as he could, then leaned back to where he was sitting again. "You got a name, girl?" he asked.

The woman said nothing, increasing Calhoun's irritation. "You can sit here closemouthed all day," Calhoun said quietly. "But that ain't gonna change the situation none."

That produced no more response than anything else he had said or done. Calhoun sighed. He didn't know what else to do. So he just sat there quietly, listening to the morning birds chirping, the cozy crackling of the fire, the light rush of the brook nearby. None of the sounds made him feel any better.

Calhoun rolled a cigarette and lit it with a burning twig. When the cigarette was about halfway done, the woman reached out and picked up the coffee cup. She sipped a few times. She tried to disguise her feeling of relief, but she was unsuccessful.

Calhoun neither said nor did anything except to continue puffing his cigarette. When it was smoked down, he flicked the smoldering end into the fire. "Hungry?" he asked.

The woman cupped the mug in both hands. Large, dark, luminous eyes peered over the rim of the cup. She bobbed her head twice.

"Know how to cook?"

Again the bobbing head. She sipped again.

"You want to eat somethin' tastes good, you'll have to cook it. You rely on me for it, you're likely to get sick." Calhoun wasn't sure, but he thought he saw a hint of a smile on the woman's lips.

She nodded again, and went back to slurping her coffee.

Calhoun stood. While trying not to seem like he was doing so, he kept an eye on her as he went for the supplies and pulled out what he thought they would need, including another cup. He brought them over and set them down next to the woman. Then he went back to his place on the other side of the fire and poured himself some coffee.

He sat quietly, waiting. After a few moments, the woman put the mug down. She stood and, with a sigh of resignation, she began preparing a meal.

Neither said anything while the food was prepared or cooked, nor while they ate it.

By the time they began their meal, the sun was up enough for Calhoun to get a real good look at the woman. She was every bit as attractive as he had originally thought. Her face was dark, but not as dark as he had believed. It was wide and round, with a small, splayed nose. She appeared to be short, though it was hard to tell with her sitting down, and gave the appearance of having a well-rounded figure.

The marks of brutality were more evident, too, under the harsh light of the sun. Calhoun hated to see such a thing, and it went far to undermine the hatred he felt for her because of her race.

"A fine meal," Calhoun said when he finished and dropped the plate.

The woman nodded.

Calhoun was still in poor humor, but he felt he was at least making some progress here.

The woman rose and filled Calhoun's cup again, as well as her own. She turned the coffeepot upside down. Some grounds plopped into the fire, where they sizzled and hissed. "Empty," she said.

The single word surprised Calhoun, but he quickly covered it up. "There's more where that come from," he said. After a pause to roll and light a cigarette, he said, "But I wasn't plannin' on stayin' around long enough for another pot."

The woman sat and shrugged. She looked dejected.

"I can't help you, woman, if you don't tell me nothin'," Calhoun said quietly. He leaned back, his elbow resting on a log.

The woman shrugged again. "Nothin' to tell," she mumbled.

"You could start with your name," Calhoun hinted. "I'm Wade Calhoun."

The woman licked her full lower lip. "Mary White Feather Crowley," the woman said quietly.

Calhoun nodded. "That's a somewhat odd name."

"I don't think so," she said rather defiantly. "My father was a trapper back in the old beaver days."

"What's your mother's people?"

"Utes." The word came out flat and sharp, with a mixture of pride and dismay. It was not easy being a half-breed.

Calhoun nodded again. After a heartbeat, he asked, "What're you doin' out here?"

"Nothin'," Mary said. The short answer was accompanied by a shrug.

"Hell," Calhoun growled. "You alone?"

"Why?" Mary countered.

"I don't cotton to a bunch of warriors comin' down on me for no good reason," Calhoun spit.

Mary's face was grim. If this man knew she was alone, he might figure he had free rein to do with her what he would. If he thought there were warriors waiting out there, he might try to use her to buy safe passage. Or maybe even kill her, figuring to make a run for it.

Still, there was something in this pock-faced man that made her want to believe in him. There was just something about the cold, strong eyes that was compelling to her. She fought off the feeling. Messing with a white man would bring her to no good end, of that she was certain. She had had more than her fill of dealings with white men. From now on, she figured she would stick with Ute warriors. They might not be the kindest folk on earth when it came to their women, but at least she would know where she stood, and she would be protected.

"Reckon you don't have to answer," Calhoun said. He let a little of his irritation seep into his voice. He was in a dilemma. He couldn't just ride off and leave this woman here. Whoever had beaten her might come back. Besides, without food, water, or weapons, she would be easy prey for any number of predators.

On the other hand, he sure as hell didn't want to take her with him. It would be foolish having to ride while keeping an eye on her and making sure none of her people were around, plus hunting and watching for other Indians, angry miners, and God knew what else.

"I might be willin' to help you get back to your people," Calhoun said. He surprised himself with the statement. "But I've got to know what's goin' on." He paused. "Coffee's over there with the supplies. Best put on a new pot."

Mary nodded and rose.

CHAPTER

* 6 *

Mary White Feather Crowley didn't know quite why she trusted this man, and suddenly wanted to open up to him. He was, after all, an Anglo, and they had caused her far more than enough trouble. Calhoun also looked like so many of the others who had abused her. He had those flat, deadly eyes; and a hard, mean face.

Still, something about the tall, lean man was compelling to her, winning her trust, drawing her to him. She almost shuddered, looking into his deep eyes. She thought at first that it was fear that had brought the reaction; she did not want to admit that perhaps it was desire that had caused it.

Suddenly she began talking, following her instincts and feelings, and going with it. The words came slowly at first, in halting sentences, but then she began to gain steam.

* * *

White Feather picked up another piece of fire-wood. A few more and she would head back toward the village. As she walked along, roughly following the South Platte, she thought about her life with the Ute people.

She did not entirely fit in with them, not with her white blood. She was taller than the other Ute women, and some of the men, too. She had gotten her height and lean angularity from her father. From her mother she had gotten the dark features; pitch, glossy hair; and flattish face. She was, she had thought without vanity more than once, an interesting and intriguing-looking young woman.

That did not make her life any easier, among the Utes or elsewhere. Her father, until he had died, had taken her to several white towns. There she was made to feel like an object, but of what her young mind could not fathom. She suspected more often than not that she was the object of their pity, mixed with fear and hatred.

Though she was not fully accepted by the Utes, she felt more comfortable in their camps along the Cochetopa or Saguache or Los Piños rivers well west of where she was now.

It was spring, and the world around her blooming. Her band had joined other bands in the annual spring migration east toward the Great Plains, where they would hunt the buffalo. They had followed the well-worn trail that her mother's people had followed since time immemorial.

The Utes considered this something of a festive time, but White Feather felt little of it. She was beginning to wonder where life would lead her. She was well past the time she should have taken a husband. She saw no Ute warrior she really wanted though. She hadn't seen any of her father's people that she wanted either, but she harbored some forlorn hope that someone would come and rescue her from this life of drudgery she faced in the Ute village.

Several warriors of her band, as well as neighboring bands, had expressed interest in courting her, as did several white traders. She found none of them to her liking, and she had rebuffed them all— politely, of course, in case she changed her mind one day.

White Feather's mind was occupied with such perplexities as she gathered her wood. Suddenly she felt a sharp blow on the head, and the wood spilled out of her hands. She began to fall, but was caught by a man.

As she was lifted and carried, she heard voices, but she could not understand what was said. The words were garbled, and she wasn't sure if the two men who had appeared out of nowhere were talking in some odd language, or if the blow to the head had jumbled her senses.

She was only dimly aware of being thrown stomach down across a horse. She fought against the flickering gray curtain before her eyes, trying to make sense of all that was happening. It did no good. The blackness smothered her.

When she awoke, she was tied to a tree. The pain in her head was tremendous, but she tried not to let it get in the way of trying to figure things out. She cracked her eyelids opened. Two white men squatted near a small fire. Behind her, White Feather could hear a river. She assumed it was the South Platte, considering the amount of noise it made.

One of the men started turning his head in her direction, and she clamped her eyes closed again. She did not want them to see she was awake.

She could not pretend to be out forever, though, and she finally opened her eyes. She was hungry and hoped that the men would allow her to eat. She also had to relieve herself badly.

The men stood. One kicked dirt over the fire; the other came toward her. She opened her eyes fully, but showed no emotion. She knew she was in a bad way, especially when she saw the look on the one man's face.

"She is avake, Mort?" the one still by the fire asked.

"Yep." He paused, looking down at her. "Good-lookin' piece, she is. Why don't you go on ahead. We'll follow along in a few minutes."

"*Nein*. Ve haf no time for such t'ings as dot," the other replied.

"Christ, Otto, you're about as much fun as a damn funeral."

"Dot may be," Otto Brandt said, turning toward his companion, Mort Boyer, "but ve haf other t'ings to t'ink about. Unless you vant them Ute Indians comink after us and catchink us vit her."

"Shit," Boyer muttered, annoyed. He bent and pulled the knots free. "All right, girlie, time to move."

White Feather looked up at him blankly, pretending she did not understand. He was tall and thin and his face was stubbled. He had watery light-gray eyes that reminded her a little of her father's. His sallow complexion and seemingly permanent sneer did little to enhance his disreputable appearance.

Boyer hauled off and smacked her a good shot. Her head, already throbbing with pain from the first shot she had taken, rang.

"I ain't of a mood for any nonsense from you, girlie," Boyer growled. "I knew your old man, and I know goddamn well you speak English. It won't do you no good to pretend you don't. Now get your rump up on that horse."

"Or?" White Feather asked, licking the droplets of blood from the left corner of her lip. She had deduced already that these men wanted her alive. She had no idea why, but she knew instinctively that it was for more than just sporting with her. Indeed, it seemed she had been singled out. That both worried and annoyed her.

"Or I'll break one of your arms for ya," Boyer snarled.

White Feather felt a chill slither up her spine. She

believed him. "I need to . . . go. . . . " she said softly.

"So, go," Boyer said with a sickening half grin.

White Feather turned, ready to step behind the screen of bushes.

"Here," Boyer barked.

Brandt walked up to stand next to Boyer, as White Feather turned around again, facing the two men. She was disgusted at them already, her stomach knotted in embarrassment. But she had enough of both parents in her to not show any of her feelings.

Her face remained perfectly calm and flat as she turned off her mind to what was happening. She spread her feet slightly. Moments later she felt the splattering of warm liquid on her ankles. As she did not show her embarrassment, neither did she show her relief.

Boyer and Brandt watched with leering interest. "Better now?" Boyer asked with oily, mock politeness.

White Feather shrugged.

"We must go," Brandt ordered. He was, White Feather thought, almost handsome. He was even taller than Boyer, with blond hair, light eyes, and a square chin. He spun and headed toward his horse.

White Feather knew there was no way out of this, so she climbed on the horse Boyer indicated she should use. She was disgusted with having to soil herself like she had, but she knew there was nothing she could do about that either.

Brandt led the way. White Feather, with her head

pounding and stomach roiling, followed. Boyer brought up the rear, his hot, lecherous eyes never leaving White Feather's back. She could feel those pale, glimmering orbs burning through her buckskin dress.

They followed the South Platte's northward course for four days, before cutting westward along Bear Creek and up into the mountains.

The third night out, Boyer threw her down, jerked her dress up roughly, and forced himself on her. Brandt was a little more restrained in his pace and force, but no less abusive.

It became a nightly occurrence, the only changes being that the two men alternated first chance at her. And, the farther they got from her people, the more confidence the men showed. At times, they even stopped during the middle of the day to eat—and to have White Feather again.

As she had everything else, White Feather took it stoically, not letting the men see that she hated them and would gladly have killed, or emasculated, them given any chance at either.

Five more days of riding long hours along Bear Creek's meandering westward course, they finally stopped at a small, rickety cabin, nestling among a grove of pines and aspens. The cabin was up against a cliff, giving it a solid back, and some protection. Bear Creek flowed off to one side, and a tiny, rippling brook entered it from the northeast.

A man stepped out of the cabin, a rifle in one hand,

and a pistol in the other. "About time you damn fools come back. Ach, I was beginnink to think you vasn't comink back." His accent was nowhere near as heavy as Brandt's.

"You vorry too much, Heinz," Brandt said. He dismounted and headed toward the cabin, leaving his reins dangling. "Take care of mine horse, Heinz," he ordered as he passed through the door.

"Mine and hers, too," Boyer added. He had slid off his horse, and then jerked White Feather down onto the ground. He ignored the black look Heinz Kessel threw at him as he shoved White Feather forward.

Kessel stood for a few moments. One eye developed a tic, which it did every time his ire rose. He was close to using one of the weapons in his hand. But he refrained. Otto Brandt was his cousin, and would be terribly angry if he killed Boyer. He didn't know why his cousin was so fond of the ungainly, foulmouthed man, but he was.

Kessel leaned the rifle against the cabin wall and shoved his pistol into the top of his patched wool pants. Then he grabbed the reins to all three horses and started leading them to the north side of the cabin, where there was a rickety wood corral.

Inside, Brandt snapped at White Feather. "Cook supper," he ordered. He pointed. "The t'ings you need are over there."

"Why'd you bring me here?" White Feather asked defiantly.

"Vhy do you t'ink?"

White Feather shrugged. "It ain't for what you've been takin' from me."

"Very smart, *fraulein*." He looked at Boyer. "Should ve tell her?"

Boyer shrugged nonchalantly. "We're gonna have to break it to her soon anyway."

"Ve vill discuss it after we haf eaten," Brandt said with finality. He went to a box along the wall and pulled out a bottle of whiskey. Plopping heavily on a bed, he pulled the cork from the bottle and drank deeply. Boyer got another bottle and did the same.

White Feather sighed and headed toward the small, iron cook stove to prepare the meal. By the time she had finished, Kessel had returned. The three men sat at the small table in the crowded room as White Feather served the salted beef and turnips. She poured them coffee from the extra-large pot.

After she served the men, White Feather filled a plate and a cup for herself. She squeezed between the table and the cabin wall, then went to one of the beds and sat.

She ate hungrily. Boyer and Brandt had fed her on the trip, but never very much. She had taken to sneaking small pieces of food as she had cooked on the trail. Still, it was never enough.

After the meal, the three men gathered around where White Feather still sat on the bed. She set her plate and mug on the floor, suddenly feeling intimidated.

"Vhere iss the golt?" Brandt asked gruffly.

"The what?" White Feather asked, surprised.

"The golt, the golt!" Brandt bellowed. "The got-damn golt!"

White Feather looked up at him without understanding, and Boyer said, "Gold, girlie. Where's the gold?"

"What gold?" White Feather still looked blank.

"There's gold in all these mountains, girlie," Boyer said. "You got to know where some of it is."

"I got no idea what you're talkin' about," White Feather insisted.

Boyer raised a hand to strike her, but Brandt stopped him. "*Nein.* She vill tell us in time." He looked at her with more interest than he had ever shown in her. "Und ve vill enjoy the vait."

CHAPTER

* 7 *

"They kept me there more'n two months," Mary White Feather Crowley said softly. "Each used me as often as he could." She paused. "They was none too gentle in it either."

Mary looked at Calhoun, unashamed. There was nothing she could have done about her situation.

"You ever find out why they thought you knew about some gold somewhere?" Calhoun asked. He was interested despite himself.

Mary shrugged. "Over time, it came out that Boyer had known my father back in the old days. Not well, maybe, but enough. Pa used to trap all through here, and in the mountains north and west of Ma's people. Somehow, Pa'd gotten hold of a little gold somewhere sometime. Boyer saw it, and just figured Pa had himself a cache of it somewhere."

"Did he?"

Mary looked at him, eyes hot with budding anger;

Wade Calhoun was as bad as the others. Then she let her reason return. "Nope. 'Least not that I know of." She shrugged, then added, "Brandt and the others also had gotten it into their heads that since I was half-Ute I ought to know where gold could be found up here."

"Do you?" He did not sound overly interested.

"Does it look like me or my people know where there's a big cache of gold?"

Calhoun shook his head. "So how'd you come to be here?" he asked after a stretch of silence.

"They got drunk a few nights ago. Not enough that I could risk tryin' to kill 'em all, but enough so's I could slip away. Did steal one of their horses, though. I've been travelin' since, tryin' to work my way back down to my people. I was afraid to delay, and didn't have much time, so I left in a hurry without any supplies."

Calhoun nodded. "You still hungry?"

Mary bobbed her head sheepishly.

"Make yourself some more to eat, then."

"I thought you wanted to be on the trail." She did not want to show the eagerness she felt.

"It can wait a spell, I reckon," Calhoun said dryly. He didn't want the woman to starve, and he had plenty. Besides, he needed time to think.

Mary began making herself another large portion of bacon and beans.

Calhoun was faced with a dilemma, and he did not like it one little bit. He had never been very fond of

Indians, any Indians. And when the Sioux had paid that visit to the homestead back in Kansas Territory, it had hardened his heart toward all red-skinned people.

Now he was sitting across from an attractive young woman whose blood was half red. Granted, her blood was also half white, but she had lived with her mother's people for most, if not all, her life. That made her far more Ute than white. Which meant he should hate her.

Trouble was, he couldn't hate her. She was also a woman, and a comely one at that. Despite his outwardly attempt to ignore it, he was, deep inside, a man who prized women. He could not accept a man, any man, no matter his skin color, abusing a woman the way this woman had been debased.

He also was finding out that it didn't matter to him that she was an Indian woman. First and foremost, she was a woman, and therefore should not have been treated so poorly.

The dilemma arose from the fact that he did not want to help Miss Mary White Feather Crowley, yet he could not stand by and let her fall into the hands of those three men again. *But, what could he do?* he wondered. He had no desire to get mixed up in her troubles.

He rolled and lighted a cigarette as she slopped her food onto her plate. He watched as she wolfed down the beans and bacon, making something of a mess of herself.

He poured himself another cup of coffee. Calhoun was not a man given to deep thought. He operated most often on instinct. Right now, his head told him to pack his supplies, saddle the roan, and ride the hell out of here. His head told him to let this woman fend for herself.

However, his heart and conscience told him he could not leave her to the mercies of nature or any man who should come along. No matter if she was an Indian.

"Can you afford to let me have some supplies?" Mary asked quietly, looking at Calhoun. "I can pay you, ya know." She lowered her eyes, unable to look at him any longer, though the implication was clear.

"What'll you do?" he asked evenly.

"Try'n get back to my people."

"I'll help you," he said. He did not surprise himself with it. He had made up his mind, albeit not consciously, and that was all there was to it.

"I can't expect you to do that."

Calhoun shrugged. He was discomfited. He did not want to try explaining his change of heart to her, mainly because he could not explain it to himself. "Where's your horse?"

"Back in the brush."

"Go get it."

As soon as she was out of sight, Calhoun moved, sliding off to the side, and positioning himself behind a tree to watch and wait. He wasn't worried about Mary so much as he was the possibility that she had someone with her. He could not be sure that her whole story wasn't a fabrication. It didn't seem likely, but it wouldn't hurt to be cautious.

Mary returned a few minutes later, leading a horse by a simple rope rein looped around its lower jaw. The animal had no saddle or blanket. Mary froze, when she realized Calhoun was not there.

She relaxed when he came out from behind the tree, sighing as if relieved of a great burden. Mary smiled, feeling good for the first time in months.

"Best clean those things up," Calhoun said, pointing to the fire, and the dishes and utensils near it.

Mary nodded. She tied the horse's rein to a tree branch and then went to her work.

Calhoun watched for a few moments, before he turned and headed toward his roan. He saddled the animal and then began to load the supplies on the mule.

Finally he pulled himself into the saddle. Mary jumped on her pilfered horse. "You gonna be all right?" he asked.

"Yep." She looked determined under all the bruises.

Without another word, Calhoun turned southeastward. Towing the mule, he allowed the horse to walk out of camp. It was, he judged with a glance at the sun, shortly past noon.

Mary suddenly rode up alongside of him. He managed to hide his surprise as they stopped. Mary reached out and grabbed the rope to the mule in her hand. "You got better things to do than drag this mule along," she said firmly.

Calhoun nodded and relinquished the rope. Then he moved on. He wondered if she had something devilish planned, but then he shrugged the thought off. Even if she took off with all his supplies, he could catch her. She could, he figured, have confederates, but if she did, they were the most patient men on the face of God's earth.

He relaxed and pressed onward. Not long after they left camp, the trail turned almost due east. Despite the altitude at which they were riding, the heat rose and the sun beat down fiercely.

Calhoun didn't mind the heat so much as he did the swarms of insects—mosquitoes, gnats, bees, fleas and things he had no idea what buzzed and zoomed around him. They feasted on his sweaty face and hands. Though there was nothing he could do about all the insects, he didn't have to like them.

Several hours after leaving their camp, Calhoun shot two quail. Soon after, Calhoun heard a small brook off to his right. He worked through the trees until he found it. The southern bank seemed less brushy so he splashed across the brook. Mary and the mule followed, as Calhoun headed eastward along the bank. The effort meant weaving around brush, trees, and rocky outcroppings.

Eventually, he came to a clearing right on the bank of the brook. It wasn't big, but it was grassy. He pulled to a stop and dismounted.

They set up camp as if they had been working together all their lives. Calhoun unsaddled the roan and began to curry it. While he did that, Mary began gathering firewood. By the time she had a fire going and was beginning to prepare a meal, Calhoun had the mule unloaded and was currying Mary's horse.

They sat and ate silently. Calhoun was not normally a talkative man, and he could think of nothing to say to this woman. He didn't regret so much offering to help, he just didn't look forward to its culmination. If all went as planned, the journey would end in an Indian village.

Entering an Indian camp was something he had wanted to do for a long time—but only as an enemy, to kill as many of the warriors as he could before they got him. He had never thought he would be riding into one on a more-or-less friendly basis.

Mary didn't know what to say either. She was still confused as to why she had trusted in this man. He had the same look as the ones who had abused her. Just the thought of that made her shudder. Still, he had made no move against her. That, in and of itself, was even more confusing. Most men, red or white, would have taken advantage of a half-breed out here. There would be no one to stop them, and, considering the poor uses to which she had been put, no one would fault the man.

Yet Calhoun had kept his distance. He hadn't spoken more than two words to her since they had left camp earlier in the day. She was relieved at that. She figured, though, that tonight would be the real test. She was not sure she would get a good night's rest.

Her fears were unfounded, though her wondering and worrying kept her from getting to sleep for a while. Then she heard Calhoun's snoring, and her doubts fled. She also was angry at herself for having been so troubled to begin with. Calhoun could do nothing to her that hadn't been done before. She had survived that time with the three men in that cabin, she certainly could survive an attack from Calhoun.

She awoke in better spirits, despite her restless sleep. She was surprised to see that Calhoun was up and working. She hurried to get breakfast going.

"You intend to bring some of your people back up here to pay those boys a visit?" Calhoun asked while they were eating.

Mary nodded, her mouth too full to allow her to speak. When she swallowed, she said, "Yep, I do. There's a couple Ute warriors who seem sweet on me. They'll be happy to raise hair on those fractious bastards."

"Your people likely to give me a hard time when I bring you in?" Calhoun asked. He was not worried about the possibility, just curious.

"Not if I'm with ya."

Calhoun nodded and finished his meal. As soon as he had smoked a cigarette down, he loaded the mule. Within half an hour, they had crossed the brook and got back onto the eastward-leading path that passed for a trail.

It was another hot, brittle-dry day with its accompanying hordes of annoying insects. The two travelers saw no need to speak; they just plodded along following the trail, grateful at those times when the trees overhung it, providing some shade.

Somewhere past midday, in a fairly long, straight stretch, Calhoun saw two men heading in his direction. They were riding abreast. "Folks comin'," he called back quietly.

Mary said nothing, but Calhoun could hear her moving her horse, and the mule back into the trees, where she wouldn't be seen. Calhoun figured she was frightened, but he wasn't worried.

The men had spotted him, so he just kept riding. Calhoun looked like he had not a care in the world, but he casually made sure all four of his pistols—the two Dragoons he wore and the two Walkers in the saddle holsters—were ready.

As the two men approached, Calhoun pulled to the side to let them pass, but not too far.

The two drew within a few feet of him and stopped. One—a tall blond man with light blue eyes—pulled off his hat and wiped a sleeve across his forehead. "Got-damn," he said. "Is a hot day, ya?"

"Not as bad as some," Calhoun allowed.

"Vhere are you headink?"

"Down the trail," Calhoun said. He didn't like such questions under the best of circumstances. In addition, he was beginning to have some suspicions about this man and the slightly smaller carbon copy next to him.

The man nodded absentmindedly, as if he hadn't heard. He slapped his hat on. "Haf you seen a voman?"

"A woman?" Calhoun said indifferently. "There ain't no women out here."

"This vas Indian voman."

"There ain't no . . ."

"It's them!" Mary screeched from the cover of the trees.

CHAPTER

✴ 8 ✴

"Dot is der voman," Otto Brandt said harshly.

"There ain't no woman here," Calhoun said calmly.

"Vot haf you done vit her?" Brandt demanded.

"Reckon you're mistaken, friend," Calhoun said evenly, his voice cold.

Heinz Kessel inched one of his hands toward the .44-caliber Allen & Wheelock pistol jammed carelessly into his belt. Calhoun saw it and shook his head a little. Kessel moved his hand back toward his saddle horn.

"You are callink me a liar?" Brandt asked harshly.

Calhoun shrugged.

"I am Otto Brandt," the big blond snapped, drawing himself up straight in the saddle.

"You are a pain in my ass," Calhoun said evenly.

Brandt's eyes burned with hatred; Kessel looked ready to choke. "You vill not gif us der voman?"

Brandt demanded. "She is ours, and should go vit us."

"All I'm gonna give you is a gut full of lead, you don't get on your way," Calhoun said calmly. His voice was unmistakably deadly, though.

"Come, Heinz," Brandt snarled. He jerked the reins, yanking his horse's head around. He cast a vicious look at Calhoun over his shoulder as he spurred his horse. Kessel followed him.

Calhoun sat there on his roan, unmoving, watching as they two Germans disappeared down the trail made gloomy by the overhanging trees.

Moments later, Mary rode out from the safety of the forest. She looked shaken, and near panic, but she was controlling it. "They'll come after us, sure as shootin'," she said. A slight tremor in her voice was the only sign of the snakes of fear that squirmed in her intestines.

"Yep."

"Why didn't you just kill 'em both?"

Calhoun shrugged. "Same reason I decided to help you," Calhoun offered. "Seemed like a good idea."

"Well, it was stupid."

"Maybe."

"Why don't you chase 'em now then, if you know they'll come back for us?" Mary's fear was getting the upper hand, and she fought back the rising tide of panic. She was half-Ute, she told herself silently, and should act like it.

"Can't see usin' up my horse when they'll come back this way."

"You just gonna set there and wait for 'em to come back and shoot you and . . .?" She battled the bile that inched up into her throat.

"Nope." Calhoun grinned viciously. "I'm gonna wait right over there." He pointed. "Come on." He headed toward the other side of the small clearing, and into the trees. In moments, they were covered by the dense foliage.

It was a little cooler in the trees, but there was still no escaping the ravaging swarms of bugs. Calhoun endured, watching the trail.

Less than ten minutes later, Brandt and Kessel cautiously entered the clearing. They stopped and looked around.

Calhoun and Mary stood next to their horses and the mule, holding hands over the animals' muzzles to keep them quiet.

Then Brandt and Kessel moved on again, easing across the clearing toward the trail at the other side.

Calhoun swung into the saddle and walked the roan out into the clearing, just as the two Germans were hitting the trail. "Back here, boys," he said quietly. He had one of his Walkers in hand.

Kessel was the first to whirl, since he was behind Brandt, who was hampered from doing so by the closeness of the trees on each side. As he came around fast, Kessel was trying to jerk out his pistol.

Calhoun shot him twice. Both balls hit him in the chest, breaking ribs and the sternum before plundering the German's heart.

Kessel fell off his horse, landing in an odd pile. He never had gotten his pistol out.

Brandt had suddenly stopped trying to turn his horse on the narrow trail. Instead, he jerked the beast's head around back the way it had been going. He slapped the horse's hindquarters and spurred the animal hard. The steed bolted down the curving path.

Calhoun lowered his pistol, figuring he would not make the shot good. "Well, let's see what you got, horse," he said mildly. He took off, racing after the German.

The roan performed better than he had any right to expect, considering his usual luck with horses, and within minutes, he was catching up to Brandt.

The German looked behind, as he had been doing periodically since fleeing. He saw Calhoun closing the gap, and he finally realized there was no escaping from this quiet, grim pursuer. He was not, however, about to quit. He slapped the reins on the horse's neck, first one side, then the other.

He was worried as he entered another of the seemingly interminable glades. It was in such a place that he was most vulnerable. He tried to get even more speed from the rapidly tiring horse.

Calhoun burst into the meadow and saw Brandt about halfway across it. He jerked the roan to a halt. He still had the Walker in hand, and he brought the big pistol up as the horse stopped, firing off two shots.

Brandt jerked as the heavy balls, pushed by a good dose of powder, smacked into his back; one fairly high, the other lower. He knew instinctively that several organs were damaged beyond repair. He slumped forward, clinging to the horse's neck, as the animal kept running.

Calhoun jammed the big pistol away and took off after Brandt again. He had killed enough men to know that the German was dead, though it might take him a little time to realize it. Calhoun wanted to keep close enough to Brandt to keep a watch on him. He had no desire to ride into an ambush by a desperate, dying man.

Up ahead, he saw Brandt fall off the horse. The German bounced, rolled, and flopped, until he came to a stop against a tree trunk. The horse continued running down the trail.

Calhoun slowed, coming to rest ten feet from Brandt. He dismounted and walked forward, the Walker back in his hand. At four feet, he fired the last round from the Colt, putting the ball into Brandt's temple.

The damage wrought by that big a bullet at that close a range was not pretty. Calhoun did not much care, though. He had seen lots worse. Besides, he had no compassion for Brandt, nor for Kessel.

Calhoun had not been sure whether to believe Mary White Feather Crowley. He had figured most of what she had said was true, but still, people were known to lie. Despite the bruises, she could have been fabricating all or most of her tale. Calhoun was a shrewd judge of people though, and he reasoned that what she had told him was at least fairly close to the truth.

His ability to judge people well had come in handy over the years, and he used it when he first spotted Brandt and Kessel. He could tell at a mere glance that they were the kind of men to batter and rape a woman regularly. They would think themselves immune to trouble and pain, thinking they would always come out the victors.

He could see the hatred and the arrogance in their eyes, and he had known right off that they were guilty. Despite his qualms about being so close to an Indian woman, Calhoun's ire rose when he thought about what this young woman had been through. She was about the same age as Lisbeth had been.

Such thoughts only made him all the more angry. So it was without compunction that he had shot the two men, including this one in the back. That made no difference to him. They had deserved whatever they got.

After his last experience, with the miners, he was not about to bury either German's body, even if he had thought they deserved it. Without another look at the body, he swung into the saddle and turned back.

Mary was waiting for him, watching down the trail. She had heard the gunfire and prayed that Calhoun was the one who lived. She did not know Wade Calhoun very well, but she did know Otto Brandt and his cousin Heinz Kessel all too well. She would take her chances with Calhoun.

She felt, but did not show, relief when she saw him. She tried not to smile but didn't quite make it. She turned toward Kessel's body, the knife she had taken from him clutched in her hand. The Indian portion of her blood was singing with the life of her ancestors.

Suddenly Calhoun was there, his hand gripping her wrist. "Nope," he said easily.

Mary—White Feather—was almost lost in the mists of time and tradition. She fought a little against Calhoun's iron strength. "I got to," she whispered in Ute.

Calhoun did not understand the words, but he understood what she meant, more or less. "No," he said again. "It ain't right."

"I got to," White Feather said again, but with less force, and less struggling.

"No."

Mary gave up, and her shoulders slumped. "My people'd expect it of me."

"No, we wouldn't," Calhoun said quietly though pointedly.

Mary looked at him sharply. She half smiled. "Well, *some* of my people would."

Calhoun nodded. "Reckon so. The others wouldn't, though."

"Give me his sheath, then," she said.

Calhoun unbuckled Kessel's belt, which held the sheath. He handed her the whole unit, since she had no belt anyway.

Mary was almost shaking as she slid the knife into the sheath and buckled the belt around her slim waist. It was far too large, and she had to resort to jabbing a new hole through the belt for the tongue to stick into. Then she sliced off the flapping end of the belt and threw it away.

"You ready now?" Calhoun asked humorlessly.

"Yes." Mary walked into the trees and got her horse and the mule. She mounted up and turned the steed to face west.

"Goin' somewhere?" Calhoun asked.

"After Boyer," Mary said flatly.

"That's foolish."

Mary shrugged. "Needs doin', though."

Calhoun knew she was right. It was a part of business that could not be left undone. If he had been in her position, he would have done the same thing. "You sure?" he asked, knowing the answer.

"Yes." There was a thin but sharp ribbon of steel underlying the single innocent word.

"Might not be pleasant." Calhoun didn't really want to discourage her; he just wanted to make sure she knew what she was getting into.

"For Boyer maybe." She looked back over her shoulder at Calhoun, who sat in his saddle, calmly rolling a cigarette. "I can face him again." She felt a sudden rush; she wasn't sure exactly what it was, but it left her uncomfortable.

"Well," Calhoun said, firing up the cigarette, "we ain't gettin' nowhere sittin' here." He moved up. As he passed her, he stopped and said, "Once we get close, you'll have to direct me. If you can." He looked at her quizzically.

"I can. I'll never forget that place."

Calhoun nodded and pushed forward, west along the shady trail. Behind him, he could hear the scavengers edging in on Kessel's body. He did not feel bad about it.

It was almost three long days of riding before Calhoun became aware of Mary tensing. He knew they were getting close.

Finally she rode up alongside him. "There's a trail, a path mostly, that cuts north from this one. About a quarter-mile west now. Take that. The cabin's a mile or so north." She fought back a shudder. "You plannin' to just ride in there?"

"Nope."

Mary sighed in relief. "You'll be able to tell when you're gettin' close to the cabin," she said. "We can pull off into the trees then and look things over."

Calhoun nodded.

Before he could move on again, Mary asked boldly, "You always so talkative?"

Calhoun looked at her sharply, and she fought back an itch of fear. She thought that she had gone too far this time.

"Not usually," he finally allowed.

Mary almost laughed. She would have if the situation facing them wasn't so serious. He was about the strangest man she had ever met. The Utes were, around outsiders, stoic and hard to read. However, among themselves, they were full of humor and jokes, when the situation called for it.

Wade Calhoun seemed always the same—cold, distant, distracted. Yet he was somehow still compelling, having an attraction for her that she thought more unusual than all the other things.

She shook her head, bewildered, as Calhoun advanced, letting the horse walk slowly ahead.

CHAPTER

* 9 *

The cabin didn't look like much from Calhoun's vantage point behind the trees. Still, he knew Mary must be quaking at the remembrance of the horrors that had been perpetrated in it.

The cabin was on a flat floor that spread out at the bottom of the slope on which Calhoun and Mary stood. The decrepit building was maybe twenty feet long, and as far as Calhoun could tell, perhaps ten wide. Chunks of wood had been torn out of the cabin's logs and one side of it sagged badly. Part of the roof looked ready to fall in.

Calhoun knew from what Mary had told him that there was a cook stove inside, and he wondered how they had gotten it here—and why it had been brought. Not that it mattered any; just his sometimes curious nature wanted the answers to things that made no sense.

No one was to be seen, but smoke curled out of

the thin metal tube that served as a chimney for the stove. There were a few horses in the fragile corral, and streams gurgled across the front and along one side. Birds chirped, and a deer warily edged up to the water for a drink.

It was such a serene setting, one that could lull a person's mind if that person was not bent on exacting justice for terrible wrongs. Such desires seemed so out of place here.

Calhoun stood, shoulder braced against a tree, looking down. His rifle leaned against the tree trunk near his hand. He allowed himself to think over the situation, coming up with several options.

He could just ride on down and raise whoever was inside. Of course, that was a good way to get himself killed. One simple shot through the doorway and he'd be across the divide.

Better he should wait and just drop the offending person when he stepped out of the cabin, whenever that would be. Calhoun had the patience for that, but he wasn't sure that Mary did.

The other possibility was to wait until darkness arrived. If Boyer had not shown himself by late in the night, Calhoun figured he could slip down into the cabin and take care of matters.

Of course, he wasn't even sure if Mort Boyer was actually here. He could have taken off right after the two Germans had left. Indeed, Calhoun could not figure out why Brandt and Kessel would have left him behind. He asked Mary about it.

She shrugged, gnawing on a piece of hardtack. "From what I learned of those three while they kept me here, Boyer was a hothead, unreliable in many circumstances. I suppose Brandt thought Boyer might kill me if he went with them and they caught me."

She could not hold back the shudder of remembering the savage treatment she had had at Boyer's hands.

When the spasm of fear passed, she said, "I reckon they left him behind because of that. And," she added sourly, "I guess they thought they'd have no trouble either trackin' me, or catchin' me."

"Plumb jolly bunch," Calhoun commented dryly.

"Soon to be plumb dead bunch," Mary said bitterly.

"We'll see," Calhoun said. He saw no humor in Mary's situation, nor in her desire for revenge.

"No 'we'll see,'" Mary said in a suddenly raspy voice. She would not say what she felt—that she had come to have faith in Calhoun, even though she had met him only about a week ago, and hardly knew him at all. "Two's already gone, and Boyer ain't got much longer to go."

Calhoun nodded. He figured that even if something should happen to him, or should he fail in this task, she would somehow see that it got done. She might die trying, but Boyer would not make it.

Calhoun had no fear of taking care of the job, in any case. It was just a matter of time. While it might make Mary nervous with all the waiting, it had no such effect on him.

The few minutes of thought also had cleared his mind. His only real option was to wait until Boyer showed himself. The man could not stay inside forever. Even if Boyer did not come out today, he would have to do so in the morning, Calhoun figured.

He thought of something else. "There any chance there's more than Boyer down there?" he asked Mary.

Mary scanned the scene before her. "Nope. Not unless they come on foot. Brandt and Kessel had two horses. There were four more—those four—in the corral when I left."

Calhoun nodded, accepting it. If Boyer was here alone, Calhoun's chore would be much simpler.

The hours dragged on. Calhoun continued to lean against the tree, once in a while smoking a cigarette or taking a sip from the canteen. Mary paced anxiously more often than not. On those few occasions when she sat, she fidgeted, picking at her lower lip or wringing her hands.

It was growing dusk when the sagging door to the cabin creaked open. A tall, reedy man stepped out and stood a moment, scratching himself. He wore no hat or shirt and his suspenders hung down at his waist. The sleeves of his long underwear were pushed up almost to the elbows.

"That's him," Mary hissed through clenched teeth. Her skin felt like it was crawling with insects at the very sight of Boyer. Her breathing was quick and ragged, anticipating the death of her main tormenter.

Calhoun nodded. He picked up the Henry, checking the charge and the percussion cap. He brought it up to his shoulder. Letting out his breath, he aimed and then fired.

Boyer had moved, just as Calhoun squeezed off the shot, and the ball only punched a hole into his upper left shoulder. It broke the clavicle going in, and the large, flattish scapula coming out the back. Boyer fell.

"Shit," Calhoun muttered. He hated missing a shot. He considered reloading and finishing Boyer off from here, but was so annoyed, he decided against it.

"Come on, Miss Mary," he said. Holding the rifle in his left hand, Calhoun strode out from the trees and down the slope.

Mary followed, towing the two horses and the mule.

Calhoun moved purposefully, with long strides. Boyer was scrabbling, trying to crawl toward the cabin and stand up at the same time. The uselessness of his left arm and the pain that coursed through his body made all of it difficult.

Calhoun waded across the tiny, inches-deep stream and around so that he was standing in front of Boyer.

The wounded man looked up, face ashen with agony. With a concerted effort he got to his knees, and then to his feet. He swayed and held his left arm tightly along the biceps, to keep it from moving. "Who the hell are you?" he asked, gritting his teeth as another wave of pain splashed over him.

"A friend of Miss Crowley's," Calhoun said. He displayed none of the rage he felt.

"Who?" Boyer asked, looking blank.

"Me, you son of a bitch," Mary said. She had walked up behind Boyer and kicked him in the back of the left knee.

He fell, landing hard on his wounded shoulder. He sucked his breath in and groaned involuntarily. "You!" he gasped when he had regained some of his strength.

"Me." The woman drew herself up straight. "Mary White Feather Crowley."

Boyer grinned viciously. "Y'all might kill me here, but you wait till Otto and Heinz find you, ya little bitch. They won't be very kindly toward ya after you kill me."

"I ain't worried about those two skunks," Mary snapped.

Boyer seemed surprised.

"They're worm food now," Mary said with a grin every bit as evil as Boyer's had been.

Boyer cranked his head around to look at Calhoun. "You?" he asked.

Calhoun nodded.

"For her?" Boyer could not believe that a white man would kill other white men over a squaw, even if she was only half-Indian. It didn't make any sense at all.

Calhoun nodded again. He set the butt of his rifle in the dirt and leaned on the muzzle. He spit, and glanced around lazily, unconcerned. "Reckon you got a choice, friend," he said nonchalantly. "I can kill you. Or I can let Miss Mary here do it."

Mary had pulled her knife, and had a feverish look in her dark, simmering eyes.

Boyer swallowed hard. He knew about Indian women and how they treated male prisoners. And after what he had done to this one, he would not die a quick or easy death. "You better do it, mister," he said, hoping his voice was firm. He gathered what little reserve of courage he could dredge up. "She comes at me with that goddamn knife, I'm gonna shove it up her . . ."

Calhoun spit on the man's face, which cut off the flow of words. "Such talk ain't nice," he commented easily.

"Hell, mister," Boyer said, fighting down his incredulity, "she ain't nothin' more'n a goddamn squaw. Christ, what's wrong with you to be treatin' her with such respect."

"She ain't but half-Ute. The other half's white."

"Still don't *make* her white, you know what I mean."

Calhoun shrugged.

"Well, hell, you sure don't make no sense," Boyer commented. He was still dumbfounded. He paused, then asked, "You scared of me, boy?" He began to think maybe this tall, pock-faced man wasn't quite as tough as he seemed to be.

"What do you think?" Calhoun asked.

"Reckon not," Boyer admitted. Still, he had to try something. He licked his lips. "How about you let me go out like a man?" he hinted.

"How's that?"

"Let me up and face you square."

Calhoun shrugged again. "Sure."

Boyer felt a spark of hope. He was fast with a pistol. Very fast. Not many men he knew of really practiced drawing fast, but he did. He had never met a man who could clear leather faster than he could.

With an effort, he stood. He was weak from loss of blood already, but he made out like he was hurt even worse than he was. He figured that any advantage was a good one.

"You gonna take all night?" Calhoun asked after Boyer had been standing a full minute. He still was leaning on his rifle, waiting.

"Reckon not." Boyer straightened himself as best he could. "Make your play."

When Calhoun came upright, letting the Henry rifle fall into the dirt, he had one of the Dragoons in his hand. The pistol was cocked. "*Adios,*" he said quietly.

Boyer's eyes widened considerably. He had been a fool, and he knew it now. Not that the knowledge would do him any good. His right hand darted for his own revolver.

Calhoun fired.

To Boyer's surprise, he was not killed. He wished he had been then. The ball shattered his right thigh bone, and he fell hard. He looked up, though his eyes were clouded with pain. He almost whimpered, knowing his death would be no more easy at the man's hands than at the woman's. His eyes pleaded for mercy.

Calhoun had none to give him. He had seen Boyer's plotting and malevolence in his eyes. He had no respect for a man who lived or acted like Mort Boyer.

Calhoun was not, by nature, a cruel man, but he had a streak in him that called for payment in kind. Boyer had put Mary White Feather Crowley through sheer hell for several months. It was not right that he die quickly and painlessly; he should be made to suffer, to realize the wrongs of his lifetime.

Calhoun shot Boyer again, shattering the man's shin bone.

"Christ," Boyer moaned. He was almost crying with the pain. He tried to get to his pistol with his right hand. He had to try something.

Calhoun stepped on the appendage. He knelt and pulled Boyer's pistol out and threw it. It landed with a plop, and a cloud of dust. Calhoun slid his Dragoon away. He turned Boyer over and checked him for other weapons. He found a smaller pistol tucked in the back of Boyer's pants and a knife in a belt sheath. Those weapons followed the first pistol.

Calhoun grabbed a handful of Boyer's undershirt and half lifted him. With Boyer screaming with pain, rage, and impotence, Calhoun dragged him across the nearest stream and then dropped him. Without a word, Calhoun turned and headed back toward the cabin.

Boyer, realizing that he was being left there to die, screamed after him. Calhoun paid the screeching no mind.

CHAPTER

* 10 *

Calhoun slid the Dragoon out and cocked it. Then he slipped inside the cabin. He was fairly certain no one was in there, or else he'd be dead now. Still, there was always the chance that there was someone wounded or ill inside, who couldn't get up to shoot outside but who could very well blast him when he entered.

The shabby dwelling was empty of inhabitants though, and he uncocked the gun and dropped it into his holster. Then he went back outside and picked up his rifle.

"It going to bother you to go inside, ma'am?" he asked.

"No," Mary said firmly.

Calhoun thought she might be lying, at least a little, but he figured she would be able to handle it. She had handled everything else so far. He nodded.

"We gonna stay the night?" Mary asked.

"It'd be more comfortable than stayin' out there." He pointed.

A pack of wolves was sniffing around Boyer's flailing. They would lose their fear of the human smell soon and begin attacking. Unarmed, weak from loss of blood, and with several broken bones, Boyer would not live long under the assault. Then the wolves would feast on the fresh body. Whatever they left would be scavenged by the coyotes that hung back a little.

The wolves did not bother Mary much. She had hated Boyer with all her heart; she saw no reason to change her opinion of him now that he was at death's door.

Darkness was nigh on them, and Calhoun was hungry. He had not eaten a real meal since breakfast. "We best get things ready, then," he said, reaching for the reins to his roan.

"No," Mary said firmly. Calhoun looked at her in surprise.

"You go on inside," Mary said. "You'll need to clean your weapons. I'll see to the horses, then make us supper."

Calhoun still looked skeptical.

"You've got your work; I've got mine," Mary said with a fatalistic shrug. She might not like it, but it had been that way since time immemorial, and would be until time ended, she supposed. Besides, she had been trained that way, and knew no differently.

Calhoun nodded. Guns were the tools of his life.

Without them he would have been dead long ago. As such important tools to him, he cared for them carefully. It was more important right now that he clean, oil, and reload his weapons than it was for him to curry the horses. He grabbed his saddlebags, which contained his cleaning materials, and went inside.

He dropped the saddlebags and his rifle on the rickety table. Just before he sat down, though, he decided that his saddle was too important to be entrusted to Mary. He went outside to the corral.

Mary was just beginning to loosen the saddle on Calhoun's roan. "I'll do that," he said. He didn't want to offend her, but then again, he didn't want her or anyone else handling his fancy saddle.

She looked at him sharply, anger budding. Then she decided it was all right. She owed him too much to quibble over such a thing. In addition, in the time she had been with him, she had seen the way he cared for his saddle and his weapons. He cared for them more than he ever would a person, she thought. That was a sad thing to her.

Mary realized with a shock that Calhoun was the type of man she had been looking for. She wasn't sure why; she was just certain of it. He was as hard and unrelenting as any Ute warrior. Yet in some ways he seemed somehow more civilized.

Trouble was, though she knew that he was what she wanted, she was equally sure that he would not want her. She could sense a reserve in him. At least toward her. She didn't know why, nor was she sure she even wanted to know. Mary sighed and began unpacking the supplies from the mule.

Both tried to shut out Boyer's screams. It was impossible, but they pretended anyway. At last they faded away. Even worse though, in some ways, was the sounds that followed. Wolves tearing at the flesh of what had recently been a human being was never a pleasant thing to listen to.

Mary kept her back to the noise. She had heard it before, and never liked it, though right now she thought it the sound of justice. The next time she turned around, Calhoun was gone. She watched as he walked around the corner of the cabin, carting his saddle. His back was straight, his shoulders square. Mary was glad she was alone.

Calhoun entered the cabin, placed his saddle in the corner, and headed toward the table, where he put a match to a large coal-oil lantern. Before he could sit though, he got sidetracked again. He poured himself a cup of coffee from the pot that was on the old stove. After a few sips, he decided he wanted a real drink. He was certain that men like Brandt, Boyer, and Kessel would have some whiskey around somewhere.

He went on his quest with determination. It didn't take long to find a jug. He pulled out the cork and sniffed at the opening. It was powerful corn whiskey, probably homemade somewhere. It would be foul tasting and potent and he figured that was just about right for the circumstances.

He poured a liberal amount of whiskey into his coffee and set the jug on the table nearby. Then he sat and began cleaning his rifle. When he finished, he started on the Dragoon. All the while he worked, he sipped from the coffee-whiskey mixture.

Calhoun was almost finished reloading the Colt when Mary came into the cabin, lugging a sack of food. Without speaking she went to the stove and the shelf that served as a kitchen workbench next to it, and began preparing a meal.

Calhoun watched her a bit after cleaning up his mess. She was, all in all, he thought, an alluring young woman. He wondered if she had a husband, Ute or otherwise. He suddenly realized it didn't matter much. She would not be interested in him. Even if she were, he wasn't sure he could be interested in her. Not with her being an Indian, and considering his feelings about people with red skin.

He walked to his saddle and slid the rifle into the scabbard. Then he went outside. The sounds of the wolves and coyotes had gone. Only a few animals lingered at the remains of Mort Boyer, Calhoun could see under the moonlight. He went to the bigger stream and washed his hands, splashing water liberally over his head and face. It refreshed him a little.

Mary smiled wanly at him when he re-entered the cabin. He thought that strange, but accepted it. Before long, supper was ready, and they ate silently.

So strange, Mary thought. *He hardly ever speaks.* So unlike any other man she had ever known. She decided it was not all that bad of a thing.

Mary cleaned up the dishes after the meal while Calhoun rolled a cigarette. She washed the plates in an old tub and then set the dishes on the counter to dry. By the time she had finished that, Calhoun had smoked his cigarette down.

"I'm bushed," Mary said.

Calhoun nodded. "Take whichever bunk you want," he said. "I'll take the other."

"You're not gonna turn in?"

"Soon." He turned the lantern down some. "That bother you?" he asked.

"Nope." Mary took the farther cot. She figured that Calhoun would want the one nearest the door, just in case. She didn't much want to admit it, but she wanted him there, too. It made her feel a lot safer.

She sat and took off her moccasins and leggings. Then she stood, facing away from him. She wondered how to get undressed for bed. She was tired of her hot buckskin dress and wanted the freedom of having it off. She glanced back over her shoulder.

Calhoun was still sitting in the same spot, half hunched over. He had filled the empty coffee cup with whiskey and was sipping it while puffing on another cigarette.

Mary shrugged and slid the dress off. She stretched, oblivious to whether Calhoun was watching. She simply enjoyed the feel of the night air on her skin. She more than half hoped he would turn around and see her.

With a sigh of resignation, she slipped between the dirty covers on the bed. For a moment, fear swept over her. She thought she could not breathe as the weight of it crushed her chest. She could see, feel, hear, and smell the three slavering beasts grunting over her, touching her, beating her.

Through sheer force of will, she calmed her breathing and brought the fears under control. Boyer, Brandt, and Kessel were dead, eaten up by wild critters. They could never bother her ever again.

It took some time, but she finally was able to sleep, though it was not a deep sleep. She was restless with demons and beasts plundering her body, soul, and spirit.

Calhoun sat for a while, listening to Mary's rustling around. He drank more of the corn whiskey than he had planned, but not very much really. Finally he lurched up and headed to the cot. He was asleep almost as soon as he had stretched out on it.

He was a little groggy when he awoke, but not so much so that he was unaware of Mary sliding naked into his cot. He propped up on one elbow and looked down at her.

Mary was fearful, worried that he would reject her. She had decided somewhere in the dim hours just before dawn that this was what she wanted, and that she must go get it rather than wait for him to come to her.

"You don't want me here, I'll leave," she whispered.

With his free hand, Calhoun lifted up the blanket and gazed at her lean form. "Stay," he growled, low in his throat. He felt the heat rise in him as she turned toward him.

"You in any hurry to get back to your people?" Calhoun asked after they had eaten breakfast. They were sitting at the table, sipping coffee. Calhoun had a cigarette going.

"Nope. Why?"

"Thinkin' of stayin' here a day or so."

Mary smiled at him lecherously. She had lost all her fear of him. "Lookin' for some more fun?" she asked slyly.

Calhoun shrugged. "Reckon the horses could use a rest. We've been usin' 'em pretty hard all along."

Mary was crushed, but she tried not to show it. "Reckon you're right," she said in defeat.

Calhoun nodded. He stabbed out his cigarette. With a determined, set look on his face, he rose, picked up the jug, and strolled outside. He sat on a stump, back against the cabin wall.

Mary worked around the shack all day, occasionally peeking out the door at where Calhoun sat just to the left. He moved only a few times, and she assumed it was only to relieve himself. Other than that, he sat on the stump, smoking and taking steady pulls from the jug of corn whiskey.

Calhoun didn't often feel the urge to get stinking drunk, but this was one of those times. He hoped it might help him work out his thoughts about Mary White Feather Crowley. Or else blot them out for a while. He knew deep down that it would do no good, but still it seemed like a fine idea for the time being.

Calhoun was disturbed by this morning's activity with Mary, but not nearly so much as he thought he might be. That bothered him, too. He knew he would not resolve anything, but as he felt the whiskey burning through his system, he felt a little better.

At one point, he needed to make water. Rather than do it nearby, he wandered across the smaller stream and headed toward where he had left Boyer. There were only a few bones, covered by stringy scraps of meat amid the shredded remnants of clothing. It was, Calhoun decided, a fitting end to Mort Boyer.

After taking care of his business, he ambled back to his stump—and the jug of cheap corn squeezings that awaited him.

One of the reasons he rarely got drunk was that it could be fatal for a man who lived with danger and death the way he did. Too much whiskey befuddled the brain and would not let the body function properly.

Calhoun wasn't sure how or when he got to bed that night. He dimly remembered becoming aware of the dusk, but after that was pretty much a blur. He slept heavily, snoring through his alcohol-besotted nose.

When he awoke, he felt like death itself. His stomach was twisted into a sour, bilious knot; his head pounded with a thundering like a giant waterfall.

Mary kept out of his way as Calhoun made numerous trips outside to vomit or make water or simply to suck up as much of the fresh, cold water from the stream as he could. It wasn't until well into the afternoon that he began to feel more like himself.

Finally he sat at the table. Without apology, he asked for some food. Without reproach, Mary made it and served it.

CHAPTER

* 11 *

"S o, what happens now?" Mary asked after they had finished eating.

Calhoun shrugged. He still didn't feel great, though compared with the way he had been in the morning, he was fine. "Take you back to your people, like we planned, I guess," he said. He took a sip of coffee.

"When?" Mary didn't feel so good either. She knew she had set him off on the drunk. What she didn't know was why. That bothered her, and it worried her. She still felt drawn to Wade Calhoun, and though she was fairly certain she had no chance of making their liaison permanent, she retained some hope of it.

"We'll leave in the mornin'." He sounded bored, or maybe irritated.

"I'll be ready." Mary felt like a fool. There was so much more she wanted to say to Calhoun; to ask him, but she found herself incapable of doing so. So she sat quietly, sipping coffee, trying to watch him without him knowing about it.

After a little while, she went and brought over the huge coffeepot. She refilled his cup and then her own. As she put the pot back on the stove, she nodded to herself. She picked up the jug that Calhoun had made such a dent in last night.

Without a word, she brought it to the table and poured a small dose into Calhoun's coffee. "Help make you feel better," she said. She had often seen her father take a little hair of the dog that had bitten him to help ease his way through a vicious hangover. She figured it might be good for Calhoun. She didn't want him to have too much, though, for that would most likely set him off on another drunk.

Calhoun nodded in appreciation. After a few grateful sips, his stomach began to settle and the pain that hammered him between the eyes started to ease. He rolled a cigarette. When he got it going, he suddenly asked, "Why'd you come to my bed like that?"

Mary was surprised, not so much at the question itself, but that he had spoken to her at all. It also made her heart flutter a little. *Maybe he's comin' 'round*, she thought hopefully. She licked her lips, uncertain how to answer. Saying the wrong thing, she figured, might hurt whatever good could come out of this.

"I was obliged to you," she said hesitantly. "For what you did."

"Didn't do much," Calhoun said. There was no falseness to his modesty.

"That's a lie, and you know it." She sighed. "You've done a heap to help me. Most men caught me riflin' their supplies would've shot me . . . or worse. Why didn't you?" she asked.

Calhoun shrugged. "Never did take to shootin' women."

"You do take to the other, though, don't you?" she asked with a half smile.

"Only when the filly's willin'." He did not smile, but Mary was certain he was being lighthearted.

She nodded. "Still, you could've done either of them things and no one would've been the wiser. Or, you could've left me behind when you rode out, without supplies. Could've been a lot of things you did, but you didn't. What you did do was offer to help me." She shook her head, still amazed at it.

Calhoun shrugged and sipped some of his laced coffee.

"Then you took care of the three animals who'd . . . Well, you took care of 'em. But even more," she added in a voice filled with wonder, "is that you kept me from carvin' 'em up. I didn't appreciate that at first, but I'm glad now you did."

Calhoun's lips twitched in what might've been a smile. "Just thought you might've regretted it later," he said softly, then shrugged. "Or maybe not."

"Reckon I would have," she allowed. "I don't get it, though. Why'd you ever do all that?" She looked straight into his eyes. "I could tell right off you didn't like me none."

"I don't like any folks thinkin' to steal my things."

She looked at him through narrowed eyelids. "There's more to it than that. Ain't there?" she asked shrewdly. She was relieved, having turned the tables on him. Everything she had said was true enough. Still she didn't want to add the rest—that she liked him more than a little. Coming out with such things would be too embarrassing. This way, the onus was on him. She just hoped he would open up a little.

With great hesitation, Calhoun explained his hatred of Indians. He told her simply and plainly about Lisbeth, and their infant daughter, Lottie, and how they had been killed by a ravaging war party of Sioux back on their Kansas Territory homestead while he was off leading a wagon train toward California.

Much of his hatred was self-inflicted. He reviled himself for not having been there. Had he been, he knew he would have died, too. But he would have sent more than one warrior to the Happy Hunting Ground before he went under himself. He hated himself for having itchy feet and for not wanting to be tied down to one place for too long a spell. Had he been more of a homebody, he would have been there when the Sioux had swept down on them.

He had hated the Sioux plenty for that, but compounding it was the fact that he had transformed much of his self-loathing into greater hatred of the

Sioux, and by inference, all Indians. For, lo these many years he had been comfortable with that hatred. It was easy and simple. He hated Indians and would not deal with them in any way except violently.

Now, however, that hatred was not so easy to sustain. Not in the face of Mary's—White Feather's—comeliness and suffering. He had been almost revolted when she had first slipped into his bed, but hormones and nature had overcome that. Still, when he had gotten up and faced the hot, bright light of day, he found he was disgusted with himself for succumbing to her charms.

He also realized with growing horror that he was losing some of his all-encompassing hatred for Indians. Such a realization stiffened his resolve to be like he had been. He would reject her.

After recovering from his hangover, though, he looked more clearly at his situation. He reasoned that enjoying Mary's company a little did not have to mean changing his ways all that much. He did not, would not, could not love her. Such a thing was out of the question. It was a mild shock to realize that he was certain of that not because she was an Indian, but because his love for Lisbeth still burned so hotly inside him. He could never fully love any other woman while Lisbeth was still so much a part of him.

Still, he could have his pleasure with Mary, and not hate her. It would not change the blackness he held toward most Indians. After all, he thought, trying to assuage his conscience, she wasn't all Indian. She was half-white, and that made a big difference. It made it easier to not hate her while still maintaining his venom toward Indians.

In addition, he could help her get back to her people, but he didn't have to deal with them. He had promised his help, and he was a man of his word. On the other hand, he had not said he would actually ride right into their camp with her. He would help her find the camp, and then send her in alone. She would be safe, and he would be long gone, without a confrontation.

He knew that if he rode into her village, there would be trouble, and he didn't want that. Not that he was afraid of the Utes, or anyone else, for that matter. Still, he had some fondness for White Feather, and would not want trouble out of deference to her. Besides, it would be easier for him to sustain his abhorrence of Indians if he did not ride into that camp and find out that they were not quite the beasts he was certain they were.

He looked across at Mary's coppery face, with the wide, dark eyes, and the high cheekbones. She was, he acknowledged without shame or regret, a beautiful woman. Even despite the bruises that still discolored her skin. There were other more brutal marks on the rest of her, too, he had seen.

He also had to admit that she had a good heart, too, and a resolve of strength in her that most men would be grateful to possess. She had been brutalized almost beyond comprehension, yet she retained her humor and her lust of living. It was something to be admired in her.

He remembered from the other morning the smooth feel of her flesh under his hand. He could feel her hot breath mingling with his; see her teeth bared as passion gripped her.

Suddenly he realized that not all Indians were to be looked at with rancor. He might not love Mary, but he could not hate her either. For beyond being an Indian, or even a half-breed, she was a woman, and a beautiful one at that. She had been debased, beaten, and kidnapped, all of which made him feel sympathy for her. He could not see any man treating any woman, red or white, with such meanness and disrespect.

As Calhoun sat thinking after finishing his story, Mary looked at him with compassion. She had faced plenty of hard times in her life, including this recent episode with Otto Brandt, Heinz Kessel, and Mort Boyer, but never anything like he had been dealt. Even her father's death several years back had not been this bad. He was getting on in years, and had lived a long full life. It was to be expected that he would die.

Accepting the death of one so young and full of life, and that of an infant besides, was more than could be expected of anyone. She suddenly understood why Calhoun never smiled, why he never joked, why he lived in such bitterness.

She could also understand why he was standoffish

with her. Had the same sort of thing happened to her, she thought, she would have hated all Indians, or all whites, or all of whatever the offending party happened to be. It was a natural thing.

With a bit of daring, she reached out one brown hand and patted one of his big, split-knuckled ones. It was, she knew from his caresses the other morning, a hand used to hard work, and danger. She worried that he might move away, but he did not.

After a few minutes, Mary got even more daring. She stood, walked around the table, and tugged on the shoulder of Calhoun's shirt. "Come," she said, "it's time we were in bed."

He looked up at her, and then nodded.

Mary had hoped for a smile, but she accepted the nod. She could not expect too much from him. Not yet anyway. She felt a rising hope, though, that on the search for her band that he might come around. She would have to encourage him.

Calhoun stood. He let Mary take his hand and pull him toward the nearest cot. She shucked her moccasins and dress, then helped him get his clothes off. With her eyes burning with desire, she climbed onto the cot, atop the covers, and waited for him. He was not long in joining her.

Calhoun seemed in much better spirits in the morning. But maybe Mary just wanted him to be, since he was neither acting nor looking any different.

She felt, however, like she could soar. She glanced down once or twice as she was making breakfast to make sure her feet actually were on the ground.

She did not really come back to earth even when, after eating, Calhoun said, "Take all we can use from the supplies here. Food, extra canteens, powder, lead, and such. Some of the whiskey, too," he added unabashedly. "We'll use one of their horses as well as the mule for packin' the supplies."

Calhoun sat thinking a minute, then said, "Reckon you ought to try'n find a saddle that'll suit you, too. No use in ridin' bareback if it ain't needed."

Mary nodded.

As he stood, Calhoun added, "Best find the saddle first. I can saddle the horses while you're gatherin' things."

Mary nodded again. Her hopes were dashed only a little bit. She was fatalistic enough to know that the realities of life had to be dealt with.

Calhoun went outside, carrying his fancy saddle. By the time he had it on the roan and tightened, Mary had come out and left a saddle just outside the corral. He saddled her horse, then hung the pack saddle on the mule and found another pack saddle inside the cabin. He brought it out and set it on top of the top corral rail. He wasn't sure he would need it, but he wanted it handy.

He and Mary began hauling supplies out of the house and loading them on the mule. Soon enough Calhoun decided that while another pack animal might not be absolutely necessary, since there were extra horses available, there was no reason to over-work the mule.

Within an hour, the mule and one of the outlaws' horses were loaded. Mary climbed onto her horse, and Calhoun adjusted the stirrups for her. Then, just before mounting the roan, he decided to take the three other outlaw horses, figuring he could sell them somewhere, if they found a town. If they found no town, he might just let them go.

Finally Calhoun was mounted, and the two rode out slowly. Calhoun went first, holding a rope to the three extra horses. Mary followed, with the rope to the two pack animals.

They walked across the smaller creek and then through the few remains of Boyer's clothing, tram-pling the shreds of cloth into the ground. There were no bones left now.

C H A P T E R

* 12 *

Four days' ride past where Calhoun and Mary had met up with Brandt and Kessel, they came on a town. A bold sign, with large letters in bright red paint proclaimed it to be Fortitude.

It was well named, Calhoun thought as he led the way in, seeing as how it took a heap of fortitude just to make it this far for most folks. It also looked like a man would have to have a heaping dose of it to live in the place.

It was not, by any means, a fancy town. Indeed, it looked almost as if it had been thrown up barely days ago, for the most part. The buildings were sprawled all over the flat space between two small peaks. Some even crawled up the sides of the hills that led to the peaks. A dirty stream wound its way through the town.

There were no streets to speak of, not with the houses and stores having been put up wherever the owners thought was a good site. Heavy rain for two days straight had left a muddy track that meandered around buildings, behind homes, and through the stream, back and forth. Other trails cut into it and led nowhere on the other end.

Virtually all the buildings were of logs cut from the surrounding hills, which had been pretty much denuded of trees by all the construction. Many of the buildings made do with canvas—old tents, covers from prairie schooners, tarps—for roofs or sides of the buildings.

The pace of life in Fortitude was hectic. Men raced hither and yon. Gunfire was heard regularly. Horses hurried up and down the byways, pressed to more speed by riders or drivers. Few of the businesses had names. Most just had a painted sign of wood or even canvas nailed up that told what type of business it was or what service it supplied. Not even the saloons were named, that Calhoun could see. Not that it made any difference to him. If they served whiskey, he wanted to spend some time in them.

Fortitude was an odorous, muddy place. The residents or visitors were dressed in a way that befitted the town. They wore worn, patched clothing covered in mud, sweat, grease, and blood. The men all were heavily armed, and most looked as if they knew how to use the abundant weapons they carried.

Calhoun saw few women, which was normal for such a town. Nearly all the women in town would be prostitutes, though there might be a few wives around. They usually were women who had come along with husbands and had no place else to go, or they were women whose husbands had died on the trip out here. For those, they would be married up again as soon as they arrived. Since women were in such short supply in mining camps and town, they would not stay single for long.

It would be usual for even a few of the prostitutes to get married soon after arriving. Of those, some might quit the profession when they got married; but others would be encouraged by their husbands to keep up their former line of work. It would help pay the bills when the mining did not pan out, as was so often the case.

Calhoun had seen many towns such as this. They were all much the same, whether they were in mining districts or near army posts. They all had the same impermanent, deadly, dull look about them; they were all populated by the same sort of people: prostitutes, con men, saloonkeepers, anyone who would try to grab the money from some hard-working slob who didn't know any better.

Calhoun did not feel uncomfortable in such places. On the other hand, he didn't feel very comfortable in them. They usually attracted the dregs of mankind, and violence was a regular part of the daily routine. He faced enough gunplay in his life not to want to go looking for it in some town.

Still, while Fortitude was crude, loud, boisterous, and potentially fatal, it also would offer amenities.

The saloons might not have the best whiskey in the world, but Calhoun figured it was bound to be better than the rotgut he drank at the cabin. There would be a hotel of sorts in town, maybe with a soft bed, though probably still with the lice and fleas that had been so prevalent in the cabin. There were at least two dry-goods stores that he could see, so he could replenish supplies. He saw a couple of livery stables where the horses and mules could get some grain. They had done well and deserved it.

Calhoun stopped at a single-story log building. A sign indicated that it was a hotel. By the looks of it, Calhoun wasn't so sure. He dismounted and tied the rein to a hitch rail. Seeing Mary starting to dismount, he said, "Stay here and watch over the horses."

Mary wasn't happy with that. There were too many hard-eyed white men here. To her, they seemed the kind of men who would think nothing of hauling her off the horse, throwing her down on the muddy ground, and raping her. The thought chilled her.

Still, she figured Calhoun thought it necessary, and she could understand that. The same men who would make her worst fears come true also would be the kind of men who would steal all these horses and supplies without a thought. Especially with Calhoun's fancy saddle, which was worth a pretty penny, she assumed.

She patted the .36-caliber Navy Colt at her hip. Before they had left the cabin, Calhoun had found the revolver and a worn holster inside. He made sure there was powder and ball for it, before he cleaned it, loaded five of its six chambers, and gave it to her. She had slid the holster onto her belt, with the sheath for the knife she had taken off Kessel.

On the ride between the cabin and Fortitude, Mary had felt self-conscious about wearing the revolver, but she was glad now that she had it. It would keep most men from bothering her. She was not afraid to use it, either, and that would, she hoped, keep her safe from anyone who foolishly thought to bother her. She was still worried, though.

Calhoun was worried, too. One could never trust the men in a town such as Fortitude. But Mary was armed, and could defend herself somewhat. The horses were vulnerable. It could not be helped, unless they rode right back out of town. He didn't want to do that, considering they were critically low on some supplies, and he knew of nowhere else to get them.

In addition, he figured Mary had not slept in a bed in a long time, if ever. It would be a treat for her. She had endured quite enough for anyone's lifetime, he thought.

Calhoun shoved hard on the door, which had stuck, and entered the hotel.

"What can I do for you?" asked a man sitting behind a desk. The big, young man had his muddy, knee-high boots up on the desk, and his hands were behind his head.

"Got a room?" Calhoun asked. The stupidity of

people never ceased to amaze him. After all, why else would he have come in here?

"Sure. It's what we do here—put people up." The boots came down and clumped on the floor. He gave Calhoun a look as if to say that Calhoun was a cretin.

Calhoun briefly pondered killing the big, young man, but then decided he wasn't worth the effort. "You got a real room? With a door and such?" he asked calmly.

"Yep. For a price." The man was bald despite his relatively young age. His pate gleamed in the flickering light of the lantern. Since there were no windows in the log front, the only sunlight that filtered in was through the cracks in the walls and door. It wasn't much. He squinted at Calhoun. "I suppose you ain't alone, then?"

Calhoun shook his head.

"Just two of ya?"

Calhoun nodded.

"Hah," the big, young man mumbled. "Ten dollars."

"Ten dollars for a goddamn room?" Calhoun asked harshly. He knew prices were high in places that supplied mining areas. Goods were hard to get, and merchants could ask what they wanted for whatever they offered. Still, that seemed a mite steep, even for such a place.

"That's right, friend. You don't like it, you can mosey on down the way there and try some of the other places. You'll find no better there, and a heap worst at most."

Once again the urge to plug the man rose up in Calhoun, and he battled it down. "Best be clean—and comfortable," he warned.

"And if it ain't?" The man's voice was filled with scorn. He leaned his forearms on the desk and looked up disdainfully at his customer.

Calhoun had had his fill of the arrogant young man. He took a swift step forward and slammed the heel of his right hand against the man's forehead. The man jerked back against his chair. Calhoun reached out and grabbed a fistful of his shirt and yanked the man forward.

"If it ain't," Calhoun said, each word distinct, "I'll make you clean it with your tongue."

"Yessir," the man stammered. He was so used to seeing swaggering gunmen that it had become hard to distinguish the real ones from the would-bes. He knew now that this one was real.

"I don't appreciate havin' to pay such an outrageous sum for some fleabag room," Calhoun snarled, face inches from the hotel keeper's, "but if that's the goin' rate, I'll pay it. Don't mean I have to take a load of your shit with it."

"Yessir," the man said again.

"Now, I . . ." He stopped when he heard Mary scream. Immediately afterward, there were two gunshots.

"Son of a bitch," Calhoun breathed. He slammed the man back into his chair, whirled, and raced for the door. He whipped out one Dragoon as he did.

Calhoun wrenched the door open and eased outside. He jammed the Dragoon away and snatched out his shotgun from the saddle scabbard and advanced.

He had taken in the situation in one quick scan. Four men, by the looks of it, had tried to grab Mary. She must have been nervous, and had been sitting astride her horse with her pistol in hand. She had shot one of the men before the three others had dragged her off the horse.

She was still fighting, flailing out with feet and small fists. Her elbows flew and she spit at the men. She was trying to bite one as Calhoun made it outside.

The three men were trying to get her flat on her back in the mud, but were having the devil's own time of it.

A crowd of filthy, beastly looking men had gathered. They were profanely cheering on the three men. Each and every one of the men in the crowd knew he would get a turn as soon as the first three were done, and they couldn't see why they should have to work for it. Let these three wear her down.

The three had gotten Mary down on the ground, more or less, though they were having trouble keeping her there. One man had each arm, and had another hand on her breasts, trying to flatten her back. The third man—a huge, bull-necked ox of a man—had her two legs. He was trying to spread them and hold them down at the same time. The effort had brought the sweat to his face.

Calhoun stepped up and kicked the big man in the face with all the strength he could get into it.

The man's head jerked up, as blood and chunks of teeth went flying in all directions. He turned the bloody mask toward Calhoun, eyes registering shock at both the pain and the fact that someone would actually challenge him.

Calhoun was not paying attention, though. He had whirled on the other two. Those men looked up at him in surprise. Calhoun shot each once in the face with a blast from the scattergun. The faces disappeared in a splattering of blood and flesh.

He swung back to face the third man.

The big fellow had stood. He appeared not to be suffering too much from the kick, though his face was frightful. He even tried to grin. Elton Marks was sure he had the upper hand now, what with this tall, thin, razor-faced man facing him with an empty shotgun. Marks discounted the two Dragoons. He had his own pistols he could use, but he would rather beat this nosy parker to death with his bare hands. It would be much more satisfying that way, and would make the taking of the squaw additionally pleasant.

"Looks like you're shit out of luck, pal," he growled through his managed jaw. The words were accompanied by whistles and gusts of wind through the gaps created by the smashing of his teeth.

"Think so?" Calhoun asked nonchalantly. He stood as if he had not a care in the world. The shotgun rested on his right shoulder, trigger guard pointing skyward.

"Yep."

"Go get him, El," someone yelled.

"Tear his ass up," another shouted.

"You shouldn't stick your nose in where it don't belong, sonny," Marks growled.

"You oughtn't to try'n force yourself on someone else's woman," Calhoun allowed.

"Shit." Marks spit blood and another piece of tooth onto the ground. Then he charged.

CHAPTER

* 13 *

Calhoun took two swift steps to the right. Then he spun on the ball of his left foot, bringing his right foot out to the side. At the same time, he pulled the shotgun down so the barrels came to rest in his left hand. His right still gripped it near the trigger guard. As Marks boiled in on him, Calhoun jerked the butt of the shotgun outward hard and fast.

The butt plate smashed into Marks's chest, snapping at least one rib. The blow did not slow the charging man though.

Calhoun managed to get the scattergun out of the way, though Marks clipped it with his shoulder.

As Marks rushed past, Calhoun stuck out his left foot. Marks's feet hit it, and he went sprawling in the mud on his face.

Calhoun swung the shotgun over to his left hand. He pulled a Dragoon with his right. He had a momentary concern that someone in the crowd might back-shoot him as he turned toward Marks.

Then he saw that Mary had gotten up. She had grabbed her pistol and taken another from one of the bodies. She held one in each hand, facing the crowd. She looked determined.

Calhoun figured he was safe enough. She might not be able to withstand the crowd, but she could give him warning. A swift glance had told him that it was doubtful anyone in the crowd would bother them, though.

Marks had pushed himself up onto his hands and knees. He was shaking his head, trying to breathe and to get rid of the cobwebs brought by being dazed.

Calhoun moved up and lifted his left boot and then stomped it down on the middle of Marks's back. Marks grunted and tried to rise again, but Calhoun held him face down.

"Should have learned some manners, sonny," Calhoun said with a sneer. Then he fired the Dragoon, putting a ball through the back of Marks's head.

Calhoun swung around to face the crowd. Most of the men were awestruck or dumbfounded. "Any of you other shit-eaters want to test us?" he asked harshly.

The men began backing away, shaking their heads. Then they dispersed.

Calhoun waited a moment before sliding the Colt away. He walked up alongside Mary. "You all right?" he asked.

"Yep." She was mighty relieved, not only that Calhoun had come when he had, but also because the crowd had left without causing any further trouble.

"Good." He paused. "I got some unfinished business." He almost smiled. "I don't think anybody else'll bother you, though."

She smiled, the first real, heartfelt one she had made since Brandt and Boyer had stolen her from her village. It felt good. Still, it wasn't the most comfortable feeling she ever had inside when Calhoun walked into the hotel again. She steeled herself.

The hotelkeeper was in the chair behind the desk when Calhoun entered the building. Calhoun didn't know if the man had been there all the time, or had watched the festivities outside. Judging by the look on his face, though, Calhoun figured the man had watched the scene in the street.

"Now, about that room, Mister . . . ?" Calhoun said evenly.

"Miles Kincaid," the young man said fearfully. "The room's yours," he added.

"Ten, you said?"

"That what I said?" the man asked, gulping. "I meant five."

Calhoun nodded. He didn't expect the hotelkeeper to give him the room, but he was not adverse to making the man lower his price some. Even five dollars was outrageous for most places. He pulled some paper money from a pocket, peeled off a five-dollar bill, and held it out.

Kincaid looked panic-stricken. "I can't take that," he said. His mouth was dry, his palms wet, and his heart palpitating. "Boss won't allow no paper money. Gold only."

"Supposin' I ain't got no gold?" Calhoun's tones were not friendly.

Kincaid's eyes pleaded for sympathy. "I . . . I . . ."

Calhoun relented mildly. "You take gold coin?"

"Yes," Kincaid breathed, relieved.

Calhoun nodded. He put the paper money back into the roll and shoved it, into the pocket. From another pocket, he fished out some coins. He handed over a five-dollar gold piece. "Everyone else in town deal the same way?" he asked.

Kincaid nodded as he took the money. He brought out a ledger book, opened it, and set it on the desk. "Mind signin'?" he asked. It was required by Caleb Woodman, but Kincaid decided he would not force Calhoun into it. If this hard-eyed stranger refused, Kincaid figured he would just tell old Woodman to go to hell.

To his relief, though, Calhoun quietly took up the pen, dipped the nib in the small bottle of ink, and signed.

Kincaid looked at the name. "Thank you, Mister Calhoun," he said respectfully. He handed Calhoun a key. "Back that way." He pointed. "Most of the rooms are just partitioned off with canvas. But there's two rooms back there that are solid, with real doors. Yours is the one on the left."

"Obliged. You have any preference on liveries to use?"

"Cochrane's. Down that way." He pointed again. "Next to the saloon with the red door. Tell Cochrane I sent you."

Calhoun nodded. "You serve meals?"

"No, sir. But you can get served up some decent grub over at Sellman's hash house. Right across the street here."

"Obliged," Calhoun said again. He turned and walked outside.

The bodies were gone. In the mud, Calhoun could see the trail where they had been dragged off.

Mary was alone and unmolested. She smiled at him. "All set?" she asked.

"Yep. Let's get these animals down to the livery."

They swung into their saddles and moseyed on down the way. Calhoun spotted the saloon with the door painted red. Next to it, as promised, was a corral, livery, and blacksmith's shop. A sign hanging by only one nail announced that it was Cochrane's. They pulled into the corral.

A short, stout man with a half-bald head came out of the building. He stopped and waited, his hands on his hips, and watched Calhoun and Mary coming toward him. When the two stopped, he said bluntly, "You're the one killed Elton Marks and his three idiot cronies, ain't you?"

"That the big fool's name?" Calhoun countered as he dismounted.

"That it was. And a fool he was, too." Cochrane needed a shave, he realized, when he ran a beefy hand over the lower half of his face. "Fortitude owes you, I expect, for removin' him."

"Town don't owe me shit," Calhoun said evenly.

"I'm the closest thing passes for a mayor in this godforsaken burg," Cochrane said, unfazed. "You want the job of lawman here?"

Calhoun looked balefully at him. He didn't have to say it, but he had just told the liveryman that he had about as much intelligence as a pile of tree bark.

"Didn't think so." Cochrane sighed. "We could use someone like you for it though."

"I'll keep it to mind if I'm ever lookin' for work and don't want to live more'n a couple days."

Cochrane grinned. "That would be a likelihood," he said cheerfully. He paused. "Well, what can I do for you, Mister . . . ?"

"Calhoun. Reckon our animals here could use some good care."

"They'll get it here," Cochrane vowed. "Got the best grain this side of Saint Louis," he boasted. He turned and called a couple of names. Two young men rushed out. "Here's animals to take care of, boys. Get to it."

"I'll be takin' my saddle," Calhoun said.

Cochrane nodded. "Don't blame ya. What about your supplies?"

"Just stow 'em somewhere."

Cochrane nodded.

Within minutes, one of the apprentices had the big, fancy saddle off the roan. Calhoun took it and the saddlebags from the youth. He slung both over his left shoulder. "Be back in the mornin', Mister Cochrane. Maybe."

Cochrane nodded, already directing his two apprentices at their work.

Calhoun strolled off, Mary walking at his side, having to hurry some to keep pace with him. He walked through the lobby of the hotel, acknowledging Kincaid's worried wave of welcome.

Kincaid looked like he was about to swallow the desk when he noticed that Calhoun's companion was an Indian woman. He was sure his boss would kill him if he found out a squaw was staying in the hotel, and that he had allowed it.

He sat glumly, thinking he was cursed. By allowing the woman in here, he risked the wrath of Caleb Woodman, as well as his job and livelihood. If he had objected to the woman, he risked his life. He had watched from the doorway as Wade Calhoun had so calmly and efficiently dispatched tough Elton Marks and two of his three cronies. He had no doubt that Calhoun could easily take care of him without breaking out in a sweat. Miles Kincaid was miserable.

Calhoun positioned Mary on one side of the hotel room door. Then he stood just a little to the other side of the door and set down his saddle. He unlocked it and then he kicked it open. With a Colt Dragoon in hand, he slid into the dark room. Only the smelly lantern nailed to the hallway wall gave any illumination.

He paused, leaning against the wall just inside the door, listening for any sound of habitation. There was none. He pulled out a lucifer, scraped it on the wall, and quickly threw it.

The match made a short, brilliant arc before landing in the center of the room, where it sputtered. It had been enough, though, to show Calhoun there was no one but him in the room.

He slipped the revolver away and moved farther into the room. He stepped on the lucifer, extinguishing it. Then he walked with assurance through the darkness until he touched the small table. He lit another match and put it to the wick in the lamp on the table. He turned and saw that Mary was in the room. She looked tired.

Calhoun walked back outside and grabbed his saddle and saddlebags and brought them in and dropped them in a corner. "Hungry?" he asked. "Or tired?"

"Both," Mary answered wearily. She felt good about herself, being here. She knew she was finally free of the troubles that had visited her lately. Still, the days had been long and hard, and she was worn to a frazzle. "But I reckon I'm more hungry than tired."

"Let's go, then."

They left the room. After Calhoun made sure it was locked, they headed out. Miles Kincaid looked no more happy now than he did a few minutes earlier. Calhoun didn't care.

Calhoun wondered, as he and Mary walked toward the restaurant, whether they would be given a hard time over Mary's Indian side. Calhoun figured he had done enough killing for one day; he did not want to have to do more just to get a meal.

No one seemed to pay them much mind, though, when they sat at a table in the dirty restaurant. An ugly, long-beaked scarecrow of a man slumped up to the table, and asked in a nasally voice, "What you want, folks?"

Calhoun was annoyed, thinking the man was trying to be scornful of him and Mary, but he kept his temper in check. "Couple buffalo steaks, good hump meat, not some gristly old brisket," he said. "Some taters fried up in marrow. Plate of biscuits. Coffee, hot, black and with plenty of sugar."

"Anything else?" the waiter asked, sarcastically, Calhoun thought.

Calhoun looked at Mary. She shook her head. "That'll do—for now," Calhoun said offhandedly.

It was not long before the meal came. Calhoun spent the short interval in watching the people in the restaurant. There was a certain amount of surreptitious gawking at him, which was to be expected. Calhoun also learned during that time that the waiter was not being surly toward him and Mary; the waiter was that way with everyone. Calhoun relaxed.

After they finished their steaks and everything,

Calhoun ordered them cobbler, apple for him; cherry for Mary. Mary was almost like a child with the sweet treat.

Seeing it, Calhoun's mood soured some. Despite the skin coloring, the bruises, the pitch hair and everything, Mary White Feather Crowley reminded him very much of Lisbeth. They both had the same vivacity; the same love of life. Calhoun felt the old sickness of hatred beginning to eat at his stomach.

Then Mary smiled at him, her lips coated with sugary redness from the cobbler. Calhoun almost smiled back.

CHAPTER

* 14 *

"Y ou don't have to do that, you don't want," Calhoun said as he stood and watched Mary peel off her buckskin dress. The garment had been filthy when Calhoun met Mary; it had gotten considerably worse since, especially since Mary had been thrown back down in the mud earlier in the day. The thing looked almost unwearable now.

"Don't you want me?" she asked, startled and worried again. She turned to face him, tightly clutching the soiled dress to her bosom. It covered little of her.

"Didn't say that," Calhoun offered. His voice was gruff with desire. "All I said was you don't *have* to. You don't want to, I'll understand."

"I *do* want to," Mary insisted. She was not lying. She dropped the dress to the floor and stood before him. She was ashamed of her body only in that she was covered with dirt, and because of the bruises that marred her soft, coppery skin.

Calhoun nodded, heat rising in him.

"'Course, you don't want *me*, I'll understand," Mary added. She knew she was taking a calculated chance. She wanted him with an almost desperation. She was sure he desired her, too, even if not as much as she did him. Still, she wanted to give him every chance to back out, if that's what he wanted.

"Why wouldn't I?" he asked, almost surprised.

"Look at me," Mary said, twirling slowly. "I'm still all covered with bruises, and I ain't had me a wash-over in who knows how long."

"I ain't either," Calhoun said almost defensively.

Mary suddenly grinned widely, lecherously. "You don't suppose that fella out there could rustle up a tub and some hot water, do ya?" she asked in excitement.

Calhoun nearly smiled. It was, Mary had learned, as close as he would ever come to smiling or showing any joy. "Reckon I could ask, maybe offer him a bit of encouragement, should he need that."

"Would you?" Mary asked, her excitement growing. She bounced up and down a little with enthusiasm. It created an interesting and compelling effect for Calhoun, who nodded.

"Be right back," he said, turning. It had been a long time since a woman had made him feel like this. It wasn't love, but he wanted to spend time with this half-breed more than he had with any woman since Lisbeth. That was scary to him, though he would never admit it.

He returned in a few minutes. He stopped just inside the door. Mary was standing next to the bed, still naked, with her small .36-caliber pistol cocked and pointed at him. She sucked in a deep breath, creating another interesting effect as far as Calhoun was concerned, and eased the hammer down. "Can't be too certain," she mumbled lamely.

Calhoun nodded. It had been smart of her. "Mister Kincaid'll be sendin' some folks along with a tub and water soon. Reckon you best get dressed."

Mary shrugged. She set her pistol on the table, bent and picked up her dress. She looked at it in disgust. She had lived in Ute camps—not the cleanest places on God's earth—for most of her life. But she was half-white, and had spent time with her father in some real towns. She had seen the ladies all dressed up fancy, with clean clothes, smelling of perfume and such. She didn't too often think of such things, but now she did.

Calhoun saw the look on her face, and thought he knew what it meant. "We'll get you a new dress tomorrow," he said.

"I couldn't have ya do that," Mary said wistfully.

"You ain't *havin'* me do it."

Mary smiled. "That'd be nice." She dropped the offending garment on the floor. A knock came at the door. She grinned impishly and struck a pose, almost daring Calhoun to open the door. Then she giggled and slid into the bed, pulling the covers up to her chin.

Calhoun shook his head, amazed at her playfulness after all she had endured. Then he turned. With his right hand holding a Colt, he opened the door with his left hand.

Kincaid stood there, trying to look officious, or at least important. Behind him were two young men holding a small tin tub half filled with steaming water.

Calhoun stepped back, holding the pistol behind him, so as not to scare them. The three entered the room.

Kincaid glanced at the bed, and his heart beat a little faster. He had heard stories of the lustiness of Indian women, and he wanted to believe all the tales were true. He sighed, knowing he would not find out. At least not now. As the two assistants set the tub down, Kincaid placed two towels and a chunk of soap on the table.

The assistants left. As Kincaid was closing the door behind him, he said, "If I can be of any more assistance, Mister Calhoun, you just call on me."

Calhoun nodded and flipped him a silver dollar. Kincaid grabbed it, smiled, and shut the door. Calhoun locked the door and turned.

Mary was already out of the bed and sticking a toe into the hot water. She was paying Calhoun no heed. She eased herself into the tub, a little at a time. If she pulled her legs up under her, she could manage to sit almost comfortably. Calhoun would have trouble, she figured.

Calhoun watched her. She presented an interesting picture getting into the water. When she was in, he went to his saddlebags. He pulled out his razor, which he used rarely. It wasn't that he liked a beard, it was just that he saw no reason to shave more than was absolutely necessary, which was almost never. He got the soap from the table and brought it over to the tub and placed the soap on the floor.

The room was small, and so the tub was right next to the bed. He sat on the bed, leaned over, and scooped some water onto his face. It was a good position, he thought. From here, he could both look at Mary and shave. Which is what he did.

By the time Mary had finished bathing, he had finished shaving. She got out with some reluctance, and began toweling herself off. He shucked his clothes and climbed into the tub.

Before long, he, too, was clean and dry, and had joined Mary in the bed.

In the peaceful aftermath of their lovemaking, Mary asked, "What'd you mean when you told that feller over at the livery that we'd be by tomorrow, and added maybe?"

"I ain't so sure I feel like leavin'." He was lying propped up some by the pillows; Mary was in the crook of his left arm.

"Why?" Mary's heart beat fast.

"Ain't too often I got a soft pillow under my head,"

Calhoun said calmly. He gave her just a little squeeze on her shoulder.

"It'd be nice to stay another day." She paused, then added coyly, "Long's we don't have to go out."

Had she been able to look into Calhoun's eyes, she might have seen the rare, faint sparkle of humor there. "What about food?"

"I suppose you could persuade Mister Kincaid to bring us over some things from the restaurant occasional."

"I promised you I'd buy you a new dress tomorrow."

"It'll wait another day. I ain't gonna miss it." She snuggled a little tighter against him.

Calhoun wondered what he had gotten himself into here. Then he decided it wasn't all that bad. Especially when he was certain of getting out of it, when the time called for it. In the meantime, he would enjoy himself. There were lots worse things in life than spending a couple days holed up in a small room with a beautiful, passionate young woman.

In the morning, Calhoun went out and spoke to Kincaid. Soon after the young hotel man returned with a tray of breakfast for the two. At different times of the day, he returned, bringing more food, and once, a bottle of whiskey.

Kincaid had been angry at the intrusion at first, thinking himself above all this. He was too afraid of Calhoun to complain about it, though. He changed his thinking on the entire matter when he found that Calhoun gave him a silver dollar each time, just for doing it. That was in addition to paying for everything. Kincaid didn't feel so bad after that. After all, with the price of things in Fortitude, where miners by the hundreds came for their supplies, and merchants could charge what they wanted, it was hard for a young man to get ahead. Every little bit extra helped plenty.

Besides, on one of his trips to the room, the beautiful, though bruised, young woman had rolled over in the bed. The blanket had fallen away, and Kincaid had caught a glimpse of her breasts. His mouth had gone dry immediately. He kept hoping for another glance at the forbidden flesh, but was not so lucky.

Kincaid no longer worried about an Indian woman staying at the hotel. The extra money Calhoun gave him made him quite glib in keeping his boss off his back.

The following morning, Kincaid brought breakfast to the room at the back. "Will you be needin' lunch or anything else again today, Mister Calhoun?" he asked politely, trying to see around the broad-shouldered Calhoun.

"Reckon not, Miles. We'll be pullin' out after we eat."

Kincaid tried to hide his disappointment. He had been looking forward to making some extra cash from the hard-eyed free spender. He sighed, knowing it would have come to an end sooner or later anyway.

"Anything else you'd like me to do?" He figured maybe he could pick up just a bit more.

"Go down to Cochrane's and tell him to have the mule and extra horse packed. Tell him to have Miss Crowley's horse—the small bay—saddled, too. I'll be down there directly to saddle the roan myself."

"I can do that for you, Mister Calhoun," Kincaid said firmly.

"You think I can trust you with that expensive saddle of mine?" Calhoun asked skeptically. He fought back an urge to laugh. Miles Kincaid was a big, strapping young man, but he seemed in some ways so childish. Calhoun supposed Kincaid could handle himself in a fistfight, or even a saloon brawl, but when real hard cases confronted him, he wilted like an icicle in the July sun.

"Yessir," Kincaid said with determination.

It took Calhoun only a second to decide. "Reckon not," he said without regret or sympathy. "Just do them other things I told you." He held out a coin.

Kincaid took it, figuring a dollar was a dollar. It felt funny in his hand, though. He looked down at it and saw that it was a golden eagle. His eyes were wide when he looked back up at Calhoun. "Thanks, Mister Calhoun," he said fervently.

"Get, boy."

Kincaid hurried out. Calhoun turned in time to see Mary getting out of the bed. She stood and stretched, feeling lazy after so much pampering. She grinned at him. "There's time yet," she said, smiling in invitation.

"Reckon there is."

* * *

Afterward, they dressed slowly. Mary felt soiled just putting on the old buckskin dress. It even offended her nose now; she had not noticed that before. *Oh, well,* she thought, *I'll have a nice new city dress soon.*

Calhoun hoisted his saddle. Without asking if Mary was ready, he headed out the door. He dropped the key on the desk, where a grumpy, sour-faced old man sat. The old man said nothing.

"And a good day to you, too, sir," Calhoun said sarcastically.

Mary giggled.

The sun was bright and hot, and Calhoun had to blink several times until his eyes adjusted. He and Mary walked slowly down the crooked lanes that were supposed to be streets. Few people paid them any mind. A few looked with distaste at Mary, seeing how she was dressed, and her dark Indian skin. Since there were almost no women in Fortitude though, the onlookers were all men, and few men would be able to turn a hateful eye on a woman as attractive as Mary White Feather Crowley.

Cochrane had their animals ready when they arrived. Calhoun handed his saddle to one of the apprentices. While the youth began to saddle the roan, Calhoun settled up with Cochrane.

Just before he mounted his horse, Calhoun asked, "Which of these dry-goods stores would you suggest usin', Mister Cochrane?"

"Bartleby's." He explained how to get there.

Calhoun nodded in thanks and leaped into the saddle in one smooth move. He touched his hat in Cochrane's direction then he and Mary were riding away.

They stopped in front of Bartleby's. Calhoun dismounted and tied off the roan. He walked to Mary's horse and looked up at her. "Reckon you ought to wait out here and watch the animals again," he said.

"I know." She had already expected it.

"I'll get what supplies we need, maybe even get myself a few new duds. I'll pay for a couple of dresses for you, too. Then you can go on in and pick 'em out while I pack the goods."

Mary nodded. She looked forward to having her new dress, and wished he would just go on inside and get on with it.

CHAPTER

✳ 15 ✳

C alhoun entered the store. Like every other
building he had seen in Fortitude, including the
bank right across the street, Bartleby's was a
crude log building without windows. It seemed sub-
stantial enough to withstand an avalanche, but it certainly lacked anything in the way of amenities.

A medium-size man moved forward. He was bald
except for a rim of white, curly hair. Matching mut-
tonchops gave him an impish look. Beyond that,
though, he did not look much like a shopkeeper. He
was dressed like the miners in plain cotton shirt,
Levi's, and high-topped boots.

"I'm Tice Bartleby," the man said. "What can I do
for you, Mister Calhoun?" he asked.

"You know me?" Calhoun asked suspiciously.

"Hell, everybody in Fortitude knows you," Bartleby said jovially. "You can't take down a man like
Elton Marks and not expect word to get around."

Calhoun nodded, not happy with it, but knowing he could do nothing about it. Better to have such a reputation in a place like Fortitude, he thought. It often could forestall trouble. Of course, he knew from experience, it could work in the other way, too, as men constantly felt a need to try proving their mettle against a known hard case.

"Anyway, what can I do for you?" Bartleby asked.

"Need some bacon, beans, sugar, powder, lead, cigarette fixin's. Guess I could use a new shirt, pants, and hat, too. And I'll pay for a couple dresses, too. My woman'll be in to pick 'em out while I'm loadin' supplies."

"We only have a small selection of women's goods," Bartleby said apologetically. "Not too many women in Fortitude just yet." He nodded, his optimism knowing no bounds. "Of course, that'll all change before long, I assure you. Oh, yes. We'll be the biggest city between San Francisco and Saint Louis within a year," he boasted. "Yessir, we aim to be the San Francisco of the East, as it were. Yessir."

Calhoun turned away and began looking through some tack piled on a table. He was not at all interested in any of the horse gear. He just wanted Bartleby to shut up and go about his business.

Bartleby did the latter, but not the former. He scurried around his store, still chattering. To Calhoun he looked like a desert beetle the way he bustled about.

With Bartleby getting the food goods, Calhoun looked at the rack with shirts and pants. He picked two flannel shirts and one pair of heavy blue denim Levi's. He looked at the selection of hats, but the choice was slim. Calhoun saw nothing he liked, so he opted for keeping his old one. It was a mess, but still serviceable.

He was carrying his clothing toward the counter when gunfire began outside. Calhoun thought nothing of it for some moments; gunfire broke out all the time in places like Fortitude.

Then there were screams and shouts, and Calhoun knew something was terribly wrong.

"What the hell . . . ?" Bartleby said, loud enough to be heard. He reached for the old scattergun he kept under the counter.

Suddenly someone burst through the door. "Bank robbery!" he shouted, then fell, dead. His back was covered with blood.

"Shit!" Calhoun breathed. He dropped his new clothes, jerked out one of his Dragoons, and raced outside.

He saw at least ten men galloping away from the bank. Calhoun charged out into the street. His eyes were covered by a red film of rage as he leaped over Mary's bloody body lying in the dust. Several other bodies were scattered about. He didn't care about them.

"Sons a bitches!" he bellowed as he slammed to a stop in the middle of the ragged street. He yanked out his other Dragoon and fired both pistols rapidly but steadily. Three riders fell.

Then the hammers were clicking on empty cylinders, and the remaining bank robbers had skittered around buildings and were gone.

Calhoun spun and headed toward Mary's body, jamming his pistols into the holsters as he stomped that way.

Suddenly a medium-size festering maggot of a man was in his way. "You kilt my friend, Elton, t'other day," the man snarled. "Now's your turn to get it." He had waited for Calhoun since shortly after the gun battle the other day. He knew he couldn't take Calhoun on directly, but he hoped for a chance. With Calhoun standing here with two empty pistols, he figured this was that chance.

What he hadn't figured on was the blinding, surging fury that consumed Calhoun. He was not even sure where he was—or even who he was. He was an animal, a ravaging, wounded wolf, as feral as anything that ever walked.

Calhoun never even stopped. He just yanked out one of his empty Dragoons and broke the man's face with the barrel end of the pistol.

The man screeched once and fell. Calhoun finally stopped, but only long enough to stomp a boot heel down on the man twice, once on the already shattered face, and again on the man's chest. Calhoun seemed oblivious to the ribs crunching.

Then Calhoun moved off toward Mary's body.

Fearful, stunned people cleared a path for him. He knelt at Mary's side, hoping against hope that he would find a spark of life in her.

She was lying mostly face down. With as much gentleness as he had shown utter viciousness only moments before, he turned her over. Her eyes were open, but blank in death. He held her there in his arms for a few moments.

"She was really somethin', Mister Calhoun," Kincaid said softly. "She saw them bank robbers, and she . . . well, she had her pistol in her hand . . . and she . . . well, she got one of 'em square. I think she got another 'un, too."

Calhoun nodded blankly. It was just like her, he thought. It was what Lisbeth would've done, too.

Lisbeth, he thought bitterly. He had been at fault there. Just like now. If he had been strong enough to resist this morning, they would've been long gone from Fortitude, and Mary would still be alive. Like the last time, he was to blame for this death.

He laid Mary gently down and rose. There were no tears. Never would be. There weren't last time, either. He was incapable of that. Ice ran through his veins as he surveyed the crowd. He was perfectly calm, but those close to him could see death in his eyes. There would be hell to pay for the woman's murder, and God help those who had perpetrated this.

Cochrane shoved forward. He had hurried here as soon as he heard the ruckus but had stopped to talk to people, to try to get a handle on what was happening. He stopped in front of Calhoun. "I'm sorry, Mister Calhoun," he said. He meant it, but he also knew there was much to be done. He could spare neither time nor sympathy on a dead half-breed.

"You're nearabout the only one here I know, even if it's just a bit," Calhoun said flatly. "And the only one I can trust. I want you to see that Mary gets a proper buryin'."

"But she's an Indian," Cochrane protested mildly.

"Her pa was white."

Cochrane nodded.

"Make sure it's done right. And I want a stone for her grave, too."

"You can pay for this?" Cochrane asked. He had to think of practical matters.

"I can pay," Calhoun said coldly.

Cochrane pulled a piece of paper and a pencil out of a pocket. "What's the name?"

"Mary White Feather Crowley."

"You say Crowley?" a man demanded, shoving forward.

Calhoun turned dull eyes on a short, wiry, grizzled old man. "Yep."

"Would her pa be Barefoot John Crowley?"

"She said that."

The man thrust out his hand. "Name's George Peckham. I used to trap with Barefoot John back in the old days, twenty year ago or more. Him and me raised hair on a passel of Blackfeet and other red

Injins, boy, or I wouldn't say so. Waugh! Shinin' times they were."

He spit out a thick stream of tobacco juice. "Where away is Barefoot these days?"

"Mary said he went under a couple years ago. Never did say how."

"Shit. Hope it was fightin' some red sons a bitches." He spit again. "Well, you just leave this here leetle gal to me, Mister Calhoun," he said firmly. "I'll see to it she's buried proper."

Calhoun looked at him skeptically. Though he seemed dulled by all that had happened, his mind was working on several levels. On one, he was sifting through what needed to be done here before he could set out after the miscreants who had done this. On another, he was talking and acting normally, dealing with the things right to hand. On still another, he was letting the rage simmer and grow, developing into a cancer that would not let him rest until the young woman's death was avenged.

Calhoun did not know if he could trust Peckham, and he said such.

"I've had a heap of men call me a liar in my life, son," Peckham said evenly, though his tone was hard. "Ain't a one of 'em left alive to do it a second time."

"I ain't called you a liar. All I said was I didn't know as if I could trust you."

"You think I'm gonna plunder the body?"

Calhoun shrugged. "Hell if I know. But I do know that I don't know you from Adam."

"Anything I can do to convince ye?" Peckham asked seriously.

"Give me your word." Calhoun decided the man was on the up and up.

"You got my word, son."

Calhoun nodded. After a second he said, "You prove false," he said harshly, "and you'll be joinin' them ones who called you a liar."

"Hell, I ain't worried about that."

Calhoun nodded again. He was certain now that Peckham would do as he had promised.

Cochrane was relieved. As nominal mayor of Fortitude, he would have to gather up a posse and head out after the killers. He did not want to be saddled with burying some half-breed first.

"You'll be joinin' our posse, Mister Calhoun?" Cochrane asked.

"No," Calhoun said flatly.

Cochrane's eyes raised in surprise. Other folks reacted similarly.

"Those bastards are mine," Calhoun said simply.

Cochrane shuddered. He would hate to be any of the men who had just robbed the Fortitude bank and killed four people in the doing. Not with this unyielding, bloodthirsty man on his trail. He had to present a strong front, though. "Your lady wasn't the only one killed here today, you know."

"I know."

Cochrane realized that argument would be futile. Besides, this way he wouldn't have to risk any other lives. "Anything I can do to help?" he asked. His voice cracked. He was suddenly scared just being in the presence of Wade Calhoun.

"Buy my animals."

"All of 'em?"

"All but the roan and the mule. The saddle on the bay, too."

"I can do that," Cochrane said firmly. He wanted to get this business deal over with. He figured the sooner this deal was concluded, the sooner Calhoun would ride out of Fortitude. Forever. "Anything else?"

"Tell me who it was that done this."

"Ain't absolutely certain," Cochrane said. "But I believe it was Mitch Dunleavy's bunch. Let me talk to some people, see what else I can find out." He paused. "You can take Miss Crowley over to the undertaker's."

"You got ten minutes."

Cochrane nodded and waved a hand. As his two assistants hurried up, he moved off. The two youths took Mary's horse, and the three extra horses, including the one with the supplies. "You need any of this, Mister Calhoun?" one of the apprentices asked fearfully, pointing to the supplies on the horse.

"No." Calhoun bent and gently lifted Mary's corpse. She was so small, so light, it was a wonder to him. He rose and jerked his head toward his horse and the mule.

Peckham nodded and took the reins. As Calhoun walked away, Peckham followed, towing the two animals.

At the undertaker's, Calhoun put Mary on a table. With a sigh, he slid his hand over her face, shutting her eyelids. Then he went outside to wait.

Ten minutes later, Cochrane came up. Without preliminary, he said, "I was right. It was Dunleavy's bunch. There was eleven of 'em came ridin' in; seven ridin' out. Your Mary got one, and you got three." He paused, took a deep breath, and plunged on. "We don't know all of 'em, but we do know that three old hands of Dunleavy's are with him. One's known as Peaches, another as Fatback. Nobody seems to know any other names for 'em."

Calhoun nodded. "Anybody else?"

"Matt Dandridge and Lymon Sharp are the only other two we're sure of."

"Know anything about 'em?"

Cochrane shrugged. "Dunleavy's a real bastard. A real hard case. Fatback's a maniac." Cochrane shuddered. He thought Fatback and Calhoun would be a good match. He'd like to see that, though he sure as hell wouldn't want to get in the middle of it.

CHAPTER

* 16 *

It took more time than Calhoun wanted to spend to complete his business in Fortitude. Calhoun half suspected that Cochrane wanted to delay his departure, but he couldn't figure out why, unless it was to give the outlaws more time to get away.

He didn't think that likely though. He figured Cochrane would just as soon see him catch Dunleavy's gang quick. The gang would either kill him, or Calhoun would extract his vengeance and then ride on. Either way, Cochrane and the town of Fortitude would be rid of Calhoun, and possibly the Dunleavy bunch, too.

One of the things that had taken extra time was having someone make up some hastily done sketches of the men he was chasing. He had not gotten a clear look at any of them, and he did not want to miss any of the seven by not knowing what they looked like.

There was a good chance that the men—who had gotten more than ten thousand dollars in gold from the bank—would split up as soon as they thought they had left pursuit behind. If they did that, they would be harder than hell to track down, Calhoun knew.

So he fretted and chaffed inwardly, while remaining outwardly calm, as the drawings were made.

Another thing that had taken time was convincing the town—mainly through convincing Cochrane— that he was better off trailing the outlaws alone. None of the townsmen, or miners who frequented Fortitude really wanted to go out chasing men such as Dunleavy, but it was their gold that had been taken. Ten thousand dollars was a fortune by their lights, and they wanted it back.

Calhoun promised that he would return with the gold, but the men were skeptical, and with good reason. That much money could make a thief out of almost anyone.

Calhoun, not much of a talker to begin with, quickly tired of speaking, and finally just said to the men, "If I find those bastards, I'll bring the money back. I give you my word. You'll just have to accept that."

"Why should we?" one man had asked.

Calhoun glared at him, but Cochrane answered. "Mister Calhoun has more reason than most of you to find those men. All most of you have lost is some gold. There's plenty more of that out here in these hills. But they killed his woman. She can't be replaced. I believe him."

"I say we send someone with him," another man suggested.

"We could take a posse, if you want," Cochrane said, shaking his head, "but that ain't gonna make it any easier to catch those men. And if you doubt Mister Calhoun's word about coming back with the gold, what makes you think he wouldn't just put a bullet in whoever went with him?"

The men growled and snapped, but in the end they were convinced. Well, maybe not convinced, but at least they had accepted the decision.

Finally everything was done, though, and with seven pencil sketches and another two hundred fifty dollars in gold in his saddlebags, Calhoun swung onto the roan.

"You sure you don't need no cash to pay for Mary's buryin', Mister Peckham?" Calhoun asked from his position up on the horse.

"I'm sure, goddamn it," Peckham snapped. "It's the least I can do for ol' Barefoot. Hell, once we was in a scrape with the goddamn Sioux up along the Upper Missouri. Thought my ass was gone beaver that time, but ol' Barefoot pulled my nuts out of the fire, sure as hell." He laughed, the sound crackling with humor.

If Calhoun hadn't been so bitter and filled with fury, he might have enjoyed the old mountain man's banter.

"I'll be back to see the grave, once I've taken care of business." Without waiting for a reply, he turned the horse and rode swiftly out of the corral. He finally made it past the last of the buildings of Fortitude, and was alone with his black, bile-laced thoughts.

The gang had ridden out of Fortitude to the north, but Calhoun knew they didn't have to keep going that way. He stopped soon after getting out of town, and dismounted. He spent nearly a half hour inspecting the ground, the trees that lined the trail, the brush where the road forked.

Finally he picked up the trail. They had cut off at the fork, heading northwest. "Best ride hard, boys," he muttered, "for your time's runnin' short."

They must have been following the advice of his thoughts, since he did not seem to be catching up to them. He thought they would ride hard for an hour or so and then slow it down. With only about an hour or so head start on him, he figured he would be able to catch them soon. But at the pace they were keeping, it was apparent that they didn't care any more for their animals than they did for people.

Calhoun finally gave it up for the night once darkness had come. He pulled into a copse just off the trail. Knowing he had to eat, he made a fire and cooked some salted beef. He washed it down with water from his canteen, but then decided he needed something else. He got a bottle of whiskey from the supplies and sat back down with a cigarette.

After a couple of swallows of the sharp rye whiskey, he decided he had enough. He knew damned well, from experience, that the whiskey would not make his pain or rage go away. He also needed to be clearheaded in the morning, since he fully expected to meet up with Dunleavy's bunch then.

As he tried to get to sleep, he battled the hell-hounds that rampaged through his hate-filled mind. It did not make for a restful night, but he didn't much care.

He woke early, sweating from another nightmare, this one where women were dying by the dozens all around him. Grinning thugs raped the women before shooting them. And all the while, Calhoun stood firing empty Colt Dragoons time after time. He could not seem to reload them. No matter how much powder he poured down each cylinder, no matter how many lead balls he rammed down into the revolvers, they fired empty each and every time.

He rinsed his mouth with whiskey and spit it out. It did nothing to improve his mood. Neither did the hasty, hardly tasted breakfast. Growling like a wounded bear, he saddled his horse and loaded the mule. He rode out, leaving the small fire burning. He didn't much give a damn if the whole forest burned down.

He pressed on, stopping only rarely to let the horse and mule slurp down a little water from a pool or brook. He ate and drank while he rode, seeing no reason to stop for it.

Along about midday, he saw more sign of the men, and he figured he was getting close. Something seemed odd to Calhoun, though. Some of the sign seemed a little fresher than others.

He came around a curve in the trail. His hat went sailing off before he heard the shot that had sent it flying. Without hesitation, he flung himself off the side of the horse. He landed hard on his hip and winched. The horse kept going, picking up speed.

"Shit," Calhoun cursed. He rolled several times, until he was under the cover of some brush. He came to a stop with a Dragoon in hand. He waited, trying to ignore the insects that danced around his sweating head.

The roan finally slowed and then halted fifty yards down the trail. Calhoun still waited, watching. The mule cropped grass at the side of the trail right nearby.

Suddenly a figure darted out of the foliage next to the roan. The man leaped on the animal's back and jabbed spurs into the horse's sides.

Calhoun fired.

The horse reared a little. Calhoun swore as he knew his bullet had struck the steed in the side. As the roan came down, it went all the way to its front knees.

The man tried to spur the horse again, but the roan was having trouble getting back up. It finally did and lurched on a few steps.

Calhoun fired twice more. One ball hit the man in the left leg; the other in the side of the back. The man weaved in the saddle, trying to hold on, while still jabbing his spurs mercilessly into the animal's sides.

The roan fell, and the man rolled off to the side. Calhoun jumped up and ran, crouched over, toward the man. If there was one man out there, there might also be others, he figured. Then he was kneeling next to the man, muzzle of his Dragoon pressed against the back of his head.

"Who are you?" he asked harshly.

"Timmy McHugh," the man gasped.

Calhoun half rose and flopped the man over onto his back.

McHugh was young, maybe not even twenty yet. He had peach fuzz covering his face, and a load of pain in his eyes. Calhoun did not feel sorry for him, especially when he thought he recognized the man. He didn't know McHugh, but he was certain McHugh's likeness was on one of the pieces of paper in Calhoun's saddlebags.

"You ride with Dunleavy?" he demanded.

"Yeah."

"Where's the others?"

"Up the trail a ways, I expect." McHugh was having trouble breathing. When he finally seemed to catch up, he added, "My horse come up lame. The others left me behind to make out as I could. If I got another horse, I was to meet the others later. When you come along, I figured I had me a new horse." He coughed, a harsh, racking sound.

"Where was you supposed to meet them?" Calhoun asked harshly. He knew McHugh didn't have long, and he wanted as much information out of him as he could get.

It was already too late, though. McHugh coughed and choked a few more times. His chest had a short sharp spasm, and then he was dead.

Calhoun stood and looked at the roan. The horse would never be ridden again. His legs kicked feebly. "Shit," Calhoun breathed. He shot the horse, putting an end to its misery.

With a replenished sense of futility, Calhoun worked his saddle off the dead horse. He lugged it back to where the mule still grazed in ornery solitude. Many men Calhoun knew had a tendency to tie the rope of their pack mules to their saddle horn of their horse. Calhoun had never subscribed to such a thing. He was glad now that he didn't.

With some reluctance, he went through the supplies, tossing away those he figured he could do without. Then he threw the fancy saddle on the mule and tightened it. He draped burlap sacks of supplies over the saddle horn. He mounted the mule and rode onward.

He felt like a complete idiot sitting in that high-class Mexican saddle with its silver trimwork on top of a dumpy, ugly mule. Still, he figured it was better than walking.

Calhoun knew, though, that while this mule would probably ride longer on less feed and care than a horse, it would not be persuaded to move very fast. Such a thought annoyed Calhoun, considering that he wanted to make tracks and catch Dunleavy's men as quickly as possible.

He sighed. Wishing it was so would not change it. He would find all remaining six men, including Dunleavy himself, if it took the rest of his days. He had nothing better to do with his life. He could devote it to tracking down these murderous sons of bitches.

As he rode, he reached into the saddlebags and pulled out the hastily made wanted posters. He culled through them until he found McHugh's. It was one of the ones without a name attached. He crumpled it and stuffed it back into the saddlebag. He folded the others neatly and slid them into his shirt pocket. His encounter with McHugh made him realize that he didn't want to be without the drawings.

Just in case, though, he pulled out the papers periodically as he rode, and gazed at them, wanting to affix each likeness in his mind. That way, if anything ever happened to the drawings, he would still know his quarry when he found them.

A storm blew in that afternoon, and the sheets of rain, heavy winds, and crackling lightning soon drove him to seek shelter. The best he could find though was under an overhanging rock. The outcropping jutted out from a cliff, forming something of a roof. Thick pines all around helped provide cover.

He managed to gather up enough dry wood for a small fire. He unpacked the mule and covered the supplies with a canvas tarp. He made sure his saddle was out of the way of any pooling water.

He sat out the storm for three days, chafing at the time lost. He only hoped that Dunleavy and the others were also sitting it out somewhere, not making any progress.

Still, even when he did get back on the trail, it was slow going. The mule was fractious, and more than once Calhoun considered shooting the animal and being done with it. But he persevered.

The rains had washed out all signs of Dunleavy's trail, and that slowed Calhoun even more as he tried to pick up the track again. Two days later, he found the spot where they had waited out the storm. From all indications, they had themselves a whoop-up of a time. Empty whiskey bottles and other assorted pieces of junk—including a number of empty air-tights of peaches—were strewn about. There was little clue as to where they had gone.

At each side trail, Calhoun had to explore it a ways, then decide whether, in the absence of any proof, the outlaws had gone that way or not. He worked on instinct, mostly, making his decision based on what he had learned in the many other instances he had done this. He was, in his career,

right more often than not, but there was no way to
know just yet if he was making the right choices this
time. In addition, each side excursion cost him valu-
able time lost in checking.

CHAPTER

* 17 *

Calhoun battled constantly with his rage. Nothing he ever did seemed to work. Making it worse was the realization that he was to blame for all his problems and troubles. He was responsible for the deaths of so many innocents along the way. Still, the self-hatred served to fuel him, pushing him, driving him.

There was nothing he could do anyway but press on. It did nothing to ease the frequent urge to shoot at anything that walked, flew, or slithered. Doing so might relieve his stress some, he knew, but it would do nothing to further his quest. It also would waste powder and ball, neither of which he could spare.

It took some doing, and another two days, but Calhoun finally picked up the trail again. He was rather surprised that Dunleavy's men had not split up and scattered, with plans to meet somewhere. Especially since McHugh had indicated that the outlaws had a hideout. Most groups of men like that would have divided to throw off any pursuit, then meet up again at the designated place.

Calhoun considered the possibility that McHugh was lying, or even that he might have read more into the young man's words that was actually there. He decided, though, that Dunleavy was just plain too arrogant to worry about splitting his forces and throwing off a posse. From the little he had heard about him, Calhoun figured that Dunleavy was the kind of man to defy anyone to catch up to him or his men.

Calhoun had seen too many other men like Mitch Dunleavy, especially in the gold fields. They were opportunistic animals who preyed on others. They would let some poor saps do all the backbreaking labor to extract the gold from freezing rivers or shallow veins in the earth. Then they would swoop down on the miners and steal their gold, knowing the miners probably would be too befuddled, or scared, to put up much of a pursuit. If pursuit did come, the outlaws would plug a few miners. That would discourage not only those miners, but the reputation such treatment would build for the outlaws would keep most others from pursuing.

Dunleavy was, Calhoun suspected, also a man to not worry about his own men either. If any of them were killed, well, there were always plenty of other cutthroats roaming the mountains. Such men could easily be persuaded to join illegal enterprises.

Calhoun understood such arrogance. A man had to be confident in himself and his abilities. However, right now he didn't give a damn about how arrogant Dunleavy was. Such an attitude could be Dunleavy's downfall. Dunleavy would not understand a man like Wade Calhoun, a man who would follow Dunleavy to hell and back again, if that's what it took.

Calhoun's face tightened with vicious expectation as he knelt on the trail and inspected the ground. The signs told him that the gang was riding fairly leisurely. After all this time, they must be feeling certain that no pursuit was coming. Calhoun could tell that they had passed here several hours before. Calhoun knew he could catch them now. It was just a matter of time and not much time at that. Knowing that brought a budding excitement to him.

Helping to inflame his excitement was seeing that the men had cut west on a small side trail. Unless things had changed greatly, there could be only one place the men were heading.

Calhoun swung into the saddle. He urged the mule to its greatest speed, which wasn't very fast, but at least the ungainly beast was cooperating without protest for a change.

Two miles away, Calhoun stopped again. He dismounted and searched the ground. Within minutes, his suspicions were confirmed—Dunleavy and his men were still following the trail. Calhoun nodded and mounted the mule. He turned the animal's head to the left, and began to force the beast through some foliage.

The mule protested by balking and making a soft braying sound. "Damn it," Calhoun muttered. He hoped the outlaws weren't too close. If they were, they might have heard the mule's noise, alerting them.

Calhoun dismounted, and began looking around. A few moments later, he spotted a broken tree limb that was nearly as big around as his arm. He grabbed the two-foot-long piece of wood and hurriedly climbed back onto the mule.

Once more, he put spurs to the ugly animal's sides, trying to get it to work its way through the greenery at the side of the trail. The animal balked again.

Calhoun lifted the small log and then whacked the mule hard across the top of the head with it.

"Now, you listen to me, you goddamn stupid bastard," Calhoun snarled, "I'm a heap more irritable than you are, and I'll beat your lazy, fractious ass to death you don't get it movin'."

He knew that the mule could not understand the words, but the point had been made nonetheless. The animal moved reluctantly. Branches and thorns ripped at man and beast.

Then a small trail suddenly appeared just beyond the rim of brush and bushes. It was not a well-defined trail, and was barely wide enough for the mule to walk on, but it was a trail. Taking it would cut several miles off Calhoun's journey. If he was right about the outlaws' destination, he ought to get there just about the same time as Dunleavy's men.

He pressed on, pushing the mule as hard as he

could. He felt an urgency that he suspected was really a desire to find the outlaws and wreak his vengeance on them. He did not give it much thought, though; he just rode on, face grim.

Calhoun was grateful for the thick canopy of trees, which served to block out the harsh rays of the sun, as well as some of the heat. It kept down any noise, making Calhoun feel he was under the domed roof of a church. That was someplace he hadn't been in ages; not since Lisbeth died. She had always insisted that he attend Sunday services when he was home. He hated it but went along obligingly just for her sake. He was rather surprised that he even thought of such a comparison right now.

As he rode, Calhoun ignored the animals and birds that fled quietly before his approach. He thought about the job ahead. He was not worried about it; he just wanted to make sure that all his energies—and hatred—were focused.

He could hear the rushing splash of the St. Louis River over the tall slope of rocks well before he saw the river or the camp. He also heard an occasional faint shout as one of the men yelled to another. It all sounded so normal.

Calhoun finally stopped the mule and tied the reins to a tree. He rubbed his rear end, trying to ease out some of the soreness. The mule had an ungainly, rump-jarring gait even under the best of circumstances. None of the past several days had met that description.

Calhoun pulled out a small telescope and extended it to full length. Staying behind a screen of foliage, he looked out over the camp, which was the same as it had been the last time he had been here. Even the small sign that gave the mining camp the name Misfortune was still there, nailed to a tree.

He spotted sunlight glinting off Leo Armitage's spectacles, and saw Willard Mossback's lanky form. They were squatting at the edge of the river, working their pans. It was so boring, Calhoun did not know how they could keep it up all day, every day. Dipping, swirling, scooping, searching. None of it made any sense to Calhoun, and he was glad that he had never been struck with gold fever.

The two other miners he had remembered being in the camp were also at the river. One was named Enos Pennrose. The other, whose name Calhoun didn't know, was standing in the water. He was jabbing a shovel into the riverbed and tossing the dirt toward the bank. Calhoun supposed the man would get a pile of dirt built up and then go over and pan it.

Scanning the camp, he saw the two women, one young and beautiful; the other old and worn down by life and hardship. He had never learned their names.

The grave he had started digging for himself was there, enlarged and covered over with a mound of dirt. Four crude crosses were stuck into the heap. Calhoun was willing to bet that the names on three of them would read Chris Winslow, Hugh Stampp, and Ian Dougherty. He had never gotten the name of the fourth. He had no more sympathy for them now than he had had when he had shot them down.

Calhoun shook his head. What men wouldn't do or endure for the sake of some yellow metal. It was sheer lunacy. They would kill innocent men, or even each other, for a handful of gold. None of them ever seemed to make his fortune, though you couldn't ever cure their gold fever. They would have it until they cured themselves—or until they died, which was the case far more often than not.

Everything not only sounded normal, it also looked that way. There was no danger here, or at least none out of the ordinary. The four men and two women were going about their business just like they did every day. They were apparently unconcerned. It was obvious that no outlaws had come through here any time recently.

Calhoun did not even consider the notion that these four miners were in cahoots with Dunleavy. He had seen all of them before, when they wanted to hang him. They were not real killers, not in the sense of Dunleavy and his bunch. They were miners, simple, rough men, who worked hard. They would kill when the need arose, but they were not the types to go out seeking to kill just for the thrill or pleasure of it.

Calhoun began to worry some. There was no sign that Dunleavy and his men were within miles of this place. They couldn't be that far behind, Calhoun knew. Unless they had stopped off to take a noon meal, or to get drunk, or to rest, or any of a number of things.

He wondered if he had been wrong in calculating that they would come here. *Maybe,* he thought, *they knew I was following, and were trying to throw me off.*

He discarded that notion. If Dunleavy suspected he was being followed, he would have set up an ambush long before this. Calhoun thought that perhaps they had just decided after getting several miles up the trail that they were going in the wrong direction.

Calhoun sighed. There could be a thousand reasons why Dunleavy's men were not here, not the least of them being that they had never planned to come here and were miles away in some other direction. Just as Calhoun had known about the small trail that was a shortcut to Misfortune, Dunleavy or one of his men could've known another small path that led north or something to some hideout somewhere.

He fought back the bitter disappointment that rose up in his chest. He had expected to find his quarry here, and finish his job. There was nothing he could do about it now, though, except to wait. There was a good chance Dunleavy had stopped for a spell on the trail. Calhoun could not just turn around and leave. Not while there was still a chance the outlaws would show up here.

He slid the telescope closed and shoved it into his belt. He walked to the mule and pulled his rifle from the saddle scabbard. He also grabbed a burlap sack of food, and his canteen.

He sat with his back against a tree trunk, looking down the hill at the camp. One small bush was in front of him, but he was not concerned about being spotted. He wore nothing above his waist that would glint in the sunlight, which was beating down on the other side of the river anyway. His movements were slow and deliberate, which would not give him away. Unless one of the miners was scanning the trees over here with a telescope, he would be safe from detection.

Calhoun rested the Henry rifle across his lap and set the sack down next to him. He opened the sack and pulled out some things. He had a small yen for some canned tomatoes, but opening the airtight would be an effort, and there was always a chance the light might reflect off the can or lid, or even spoon.

He settled, reluctantly, for some jerky and hard-tack. He was plumb sick of such fare, but he could not change the circumstances that forced him to live on it for long stretches. He was glad that it was buffalo jerky, though. He had eaten beef jerky, and he much preferred buffalo.

It was a chore to remain awake as the afternoon wore on. The heat, his sickness of self-hatred, and the boredom all conspired to make his eyelids droop. The only thing keeping him awake was the annoying presence of several clouds of insects buzzing around his head.

Calhoun did allow himself some catnaps, though.

For as long as he remembered, he had had the capacity to sleep anywhere and wake at the slightest hint of danger. He also had the ability to set a clock in his head for whenever he wanted to wake.

Just before dusk, Calhoun roused himself from another catnap. He almost smiled as he saw six men riding into Misfortune. He pulled out his telescope and observed the six. He nodded. There was no need for him to pull out the drawings in his pocket. Mitch Dunleavy and his cronies had arrived after all.

With measured hurriedness, Calhoun grabbed the canteen and burlap sack and brought them back to the mule. While he was hanging them on the saddle, he heard the gunfire.

He spun and sprinted for the tree he had just left.

CHAPTER

* 18 *

Dunleavy and his crew had wasted no time. As the four miners looked up from their work in the stream, the outlaws were spreading out through camp, unlimbering their weapons.

By the time Calhoun got back to his tree and snatched up his rifle, all four miners were down. Pennrose and the one Calhoun didn't know floated face down in the slower current at the edge of the river on the far side. Mossback lay on the bank, on Calhoun's side of the river. Armitage was also on the same side, crawling weakly toward the trees that dotted the steep slope.

One of Dunleavy's men threw back his head and laughed. He rode forward, and splashed across the river. Without getting off his horse, he shot Armitage in the back of the head. Then he headed back toward the camp. Calhoun thought the man was still laughing, though he could not hear it with the rush of the river over the high cleft in the rocks.

Calhoun took a deep breath to settle the fires of excitement that had burst into flame inside him. The time had come.

He lifted the rifle and turned toward the mule. This was not a job to do at long range, with a rifle. Besides, with the single-shot Henry, he'd most likely only get two or three before the others would scatter and get into the cover of the brush. Then he would have to hunt them down in the dark, foreboding forest; or try to track them down again. Neither appealed to him.

Calhoun would much prefer to ride on down there and confront the outlaws. He was as arrogant in some ways as they were. His arrogance was fostered on his knowledge of and confidence in his abilities. Unlike Dunleavy, whom he assumed was arrogant simply because he created fear in many people because of his viciousness, and willingness to back-shoot people.

Calhoun was fully aware that by doing what he planned he could die. Thing was, he didn't care. As long as he took most of Dunleavy's men out with him. It was what he would have done that night long ago when the Sioux had swept down on the farmstead.

He was just about ready to climb into the saddle when he heard a faint scream. "Damn!" he mumbled. He whirled and ran for the tree once again.

Two of the men had found the women of Misfortune. The outlaws were dragging the women by the hair from behind a tent. Calhoun figured the women had run and hid in the forest when Dunleavy's crew arrived.

Searching through the drawings in his mind's eye, he determined that the two roughly hauling the women into the center of the mining camp were Lymon Sharp, and the only one he still had no name for.

The men argued for a little bit. Calhoun could hear nothing of what was being said, though he deduced that they were arguing over what to do with the older woman. She would be of little use to such men as these, and Calhoun wondered why any of them would argue to spare her life. He had expected her to be killed right off.

Finally the argument tapered off. While Sharp and Matt Dandridge held the older woman, Fatback, Peaches, and the unnamed man flung the younger woman to the ground with her head in Calhoun's direction and pinned her there. Fatback and Peaches each held one of the women's legs.

The unnamed man was at her head, one knee pressing hard on each of her arms. One hand was on her bosom, holding her flat. The other hand held a knife, which the man was trying to work through her clothes.

Even up on the hill, with the roar of the river, Calhoun could hear her screams, and he was sickened. He brought the rifle up to his shoulder.

Dunleavy, facing in Calhoun's direction, had made a big show of taking off his gun belt and then dropping his trousers. Before Calhoun could get off a shot at him, he had quickly knelt, putting him somewhat in back of the unnamed man. He swiftly shoved the woman's simple calico dress up well past her waist. She wore nothing underneath.

Calhoun knew Dunleavy was about to force himself on the woman. He would be fried in hell for all eternity, he figured, if he let another woman be debased when he could do something to prevent it. For him, it was not some miner's wife down there about to be ravaged. It was not even simply the wife of a man he had been forced to kill. She was, for him, the whole of all her gender; all the women who had ever been treated in such a base manner. She was all the women he had failed to protect.

The thoughts, which were unorganized, had flitted through his mind in less time than it took to blink. He had to do something, and do it now.

He had no shot at Dunleavy, partly shielded as he was by the unnamed man. Calhoun figured the man with no name would do just as well at this point in time. He fired.

The ball punched into the back of the man's head. Bone, blood, and brain matter flew. The man pitched forward, landing in an obscene position atop the woman. Dunleavy jerked backward out of the way, swearing. He fell on his back, trying to pull up his pants. He finally managed, then rolled until he had grabbed his holster from the ground and pulled out a pistol. He lay on his stomach, looking around, frantically trying to spot the enemy.

Peaches and Fatback wasted no time. They had seen men killed before, and had no love for their companion anyway. As soon as the man's head blew apart, they released the woman's legs and scrambled for their horses, hoping not to take a bullet in the back as they ran.

Sharp and Dandridge threw the older woman to the ground and raced toward the horses, too.

When no second shot came, Dunleavy jumped up. His men were getting mounted. Peaches, the only one fully on a horse, had grabbed the reins to Dunleavy's animal and was racing toward him with it. They stopped in a cloud of dust, and Dunleavy leaped into the saddle.

Dunleavy looked up the hill and saw a man charging down the rocky gradient. He snarled. "Shit, ain't but a one of 'em," he shouted at his men.

The others rode up and watched.

"We'll put an end to these goddamn high jinks right now," Fatback said. He was a greasy, sluglike man, with a pasty, jowly face that was so fat his eyes seemed permanently closed. He brought his rifle up and fired.

"Son of a bitch," he muttered when the rider coming at them never even slowed.

"Always said you couldn't shoot, you big fat tub of lard," Peaches said. He was a skinny, wrinkled man, whose fondness for canned peaches had given him his nickname.

Peaches and several of the others pulled their pistols and began taking potshots. It was almost like a festival for them, and they were having a whoop-up time.

After killing the unnamed man, Calhoun had debated for perhaps half a second whether he should quickly reload and try to take out some more of Dunleavy's men. In that flickering instant of time, though, he realized that would be foolhardy. He might, possibly get one more if he was fast enough at reloading, but that would be all.

He ran for the mule. Leaping into the saddle, he spurred the reluctant beast. "You best move your ass good this time," he mumbled.

The mule seemed to understand. It lumbered into motion. Calhoun jammed the Henry into the scabbard. The animal had picked up some speed by the time it hit the edge of the slope. It brayed wildly as it skidded, stiff-legged and half on its haunches down the hill. Dust flew and rocks rolled crazily down.

Calhoun was amazed when the mule hit the bottom and caught its rhythm right off, lengthening its strides into a hard-gaited run. It secmed almost as if it was trying to impress Calhoun with its speed and capabilities.

They hit the water with a splash. Calhoun was fairly certain the animal would stop then, probably pitching him into the river. To his surprise, the mule kept going.

Through the mists of water kicked up by the charging animal Calhoun could see the outlaws shooting at him. He paid the bullets no mind. He would either be hit, or he wouldn't. And he was not about to start firing until he was on dry land again. Firing from the back of a running animal was bad enough; trying to do it while the mule was bucking the swift current of a river would be plain wasteful.

As soon as the mule was on the bank, Calhoun pulled out one of the Walkers from the saddle holster. He hoped the dash across the river had not dampened his powder. If it had, he would be in deep trouble. He fired once, and felt a mild touch of relief as the five-pound revolver bucked in his hand.

He kept firing steadily, and when that Walker was empty, he shoved it away and grabbed the other one.

Suddenly Dandridge shouted, "Goddamn, that's that son of a bitch killed Kirby, Sells, and Slick Charlie back in Fortitude." He paused. "Jesus, I ain't about to . . ."

Dandridge stopped speaking abruptly when Sharp suddenly grunted and clutched at his stomach. A moment later, Sharp was knocked back off his horse, red spurting from his throat.

"Damn," Peaches snarled. He pulled his rifle and fired. Calhoun never stopped coming, though Peaches would have sworn that he had hit the racing gunman.

The others fired hastily, setting up a fusillade, trying to bring down the madman. Their bullets seemed to have no effect on him.

"That's enough for me," Dandridge said nervously. He tugged on his reins, trying to back his horse out of the crowd of companions who boxed him in. He was sweating from fear, which had also turned his handsome young face ashen.

Then he, too, went down, a ball from Calhoun's Walker piercing his lungs after having smashed through his upper arm.

The outlaws turned and galloped toward the trail from which they had entered the aptly named mining camp.

Calhoun thundered ahead, firing as he rode. He was pleased when he saw one man go down. His eyes once again seemed covered with a film of red as hate pulsed through him with each heartbeat.

He winced and sucked in a breath, when he felt the searing flame of a ball punch through him, high up on the right side of his chest, just under the collarbone.

Still, that did not slow him. He raced on, firing until the second Walker was empty. He noticed with some satisfaction that another outlaw had gone down. Revenge, he thought, was indeed sweet.

Calhoun felt another ball hit his left thigh, and he swore at the sudden sharp pain. He still did not stop, or even slow.

He saw Dunleavy and his two remaining cronies turn tail and race off. In his rage, Calhoun's first thought was to go after them. Then he realized that would be enormously foolish. He was wounded twice that he knew of, and was losing blood fast. In addition, there was a good chance that Dunleavy and the others would be waiting in ambush for him just down the trail.

Neither of those things mattered much to him. He fully expected to die here today. He would like to take at least a couple more of those outlaws with him, though.

What really stopped him was seeing, as he raced past, the young woman still covered by the unnamed man's body. The man was a big, hulking brute, and no lightweight. The woman's arms flapped as she tried to hoist the dead weight off her.

The older woman was kneeling beside her, trying to help her get free from the disgusting predicament.

Calhoun pulled the mule to a stop. The beast stood, blowing heavily. It was not used to such activity. Calhoun turned and walked the mule back to where the women were.

He slid off the mule, but held on when he realized he was weak and shaky. Sucking in a few deep breaths, he pushed off the animal. He walked unsteadily the several steps to where the women were. He knelt, having to catch himself from falling. He managed, but in twisting to make sure he did not let his weight fall on the body atop the woman, he sent a stab of pain through his chest.

It took a few moments of kneeling there, head down, before the pain subsided enough for him to move again. When he pushed back a little, the older woman glanced at him.

Her look of relief changed instantly to one of fear and dislike. "You!" she breathed in horror.

"Yes'm," Calhoun said. He couldn't have smiled, even if he had wanted to.

"I don't want . . ."

"Ma'am," Calhoun said sharply, "we can set here and jaw all the day, especially on my bad traits." He paused, wincing. "But I don't expect your friend here'll be too thankful for it."

"But you . . ."

"You can either help me get this piece of lard off your friend, or you can set here and watch her die, slowly, suffocatin' under that foul blob layin' on her."

The old woman's face set in determination. She nodded. She bent to the task.

CHAPTER
* 19 *

Even as weak as Calhoun was, he and the old woman managed to roll the fat, unnamed man off of the young woman.

When the deed was complete, the old woman hurriedly reached out and tugged the younger woman's dress down as modestly as she could. The younger woman nodded gratefully. She was still unable to move.

As soon as she was free, the young woman sucked in deep breath after deep breath. She was grateful for the oxygen, but more so for the freshness of the air. The man's bladder had released in death, and he wet himself. The foul odor of urine, as well as the man's seemingly normal rankness had been right over her face. She had thought at first that she would gag to death from the stench, if she didn't die from lack of oxygen.

When she thought she had gotten her breath back, she leaped up and ran for the river.

Calhoun rose unsteadily. The older woman looked up at him. "You're hurt," she said. She wasn't sure whether to be glad or concerned. She took a middle, noncommittal ground.

"Yes'm." He sat, perching himself on the dead man's chest. He pulled the top of his shirt out a little and looked inside. He had been hurt worse than this before, but with two wounds, he was losing a lot of blood. That was bad.

He also was worried that Dunleavy, Fatback, and Peaches would return. He wasn't concerned for himself, but now he was saddled with these two women. That was all he needed. He wondered how he was so lucky to find himself in such a situation with such frequency. He sighed. It couldn't be helped now.

Calhoun glanced toward the river. The young woman was still standing in the cold water, scrubbing her face. Even from his distance, Calhoun could see that she seemed intent on peeling the skin right off to rid her of the odorous remembrances.

"Best go get your friend, ma'am," Calhoun said softly.

"Why?"

"Those boys might just decide to come back here, they remember they're only runnin' from one man. And a wounded one at that. You want 'em back here?"

"Good Lord, no," the woman exclaimed. She studied him for a moment. She wasn't quite sure why she disliked him so much. He had not killed her husband. On the other hand, he had killed four of her husband's friends, five if you counted Harry Templeton. Still, he didn't really seem a bad sort.

He was a tough-looking man, that was sure. But so were so many others out here. That didn't make him so bad a man. Neither did killing four men who were not only planning on lynching you but making you dig your own grave. "You got a name?" she asked suddenly.

"Wade Calhoun. You?"

"Aggie Armitage."

"I'm sorry, ma'am," he said, working up a little sympathy.

Aggie nodded. She licked her weathered lips. "You saw Leo?"

"Yes'm," Calhoun said quietly.

She nodded again, understanding. She and Leo Armitage had had thirty-seven years together. Not all of them had been good, but more were good than bad. Even if he did have a habit of dragging her to places like Misfortune.

Aggie broke off her thoughts of her husband. There were things that had to be done. "You going to be all right?" she asked, a sudden note of concern in her voice. She might not like Calhoun very much, but he had saved her and Helena, and that counted for something. Besides, she had seen wounded men before, and Calhoun did not look good. Aggie realized she and Helena would need Calhoun if they were to get to safety somewhere. The two women would not get far on their own, she thought, not when one was an old lady, and the other a still mostly inexperienced young woman.

"I expect so," Calhoun said. There was little pain since the numbness had set in. He worried some about that.

Aggie looked doubtful, and thought she should look at the wound. She had no little experience in frontier doctoring, and might be able to do him some good. He would have to wait a little, though. She pushed herself up, suddenly feeling every one of her fifty-five years. "I best get Helena, like you said."

Calhoun nodded, not looking at her. He had pulled his bandanna off and was wrapping it around his blood-covered thigh. He pulled it hard and knotted it as tight as he could.

Aggie took two steps and turned back. She watched Calhoun at his work for a moment before saying, "Mister Calhoun?"

When he looked up, she asked quietly, "Why'd you kill Mister Templeton?"

"He got it in his mind that I was tryin' to steal his gold, and he set about to stop me."

"Were you?"

"No, ma'am. I never caught the gold fever. Don't have much use for it most times."

"But you killed him for gold."

"He had the drop on me, ma'am. Made me set my

guns aside. He was aimin' to kill me. I wasn't about to set there and have him plug me."

"Did you have to kill him?" She had known Harry Templeton, and of his paranoia where gold was concerned. She also figured Calhoun was telling the truth. Templeton had been so obsessed that she could easily see him blasting an innocent man simply on the thought that the man might be trying to steal his precious poke.

"It don't pay to shoot an armed man and not kill him, ma'am. That's too often fatal."

Aggie nodded sadly. She understood. She didn't like it much, but she understood. With understanding, too, came a new look at Calhoun. She would, she thought, be a little more objective about Calhoun, at least until she knew more about him.

"That gold was ours, Mister Calhoun," she said. "We had pooled it for supplies. Mister Templeton was to ride on down to Fortitude to buy them."

Calhoun shrugged. He pointed to the mule. "It's in that leather sack there hanging from my saddle."

Aggie looked stunned. "What're you saying, Mister Calhoun?" she stammered.

"It's yours, take it. Like I said, I got no use for it."

Aggie's opinion of Wade Calhoun soared. Dumbfounded, she turned and staggered away, toward the river. She believed him, and if he said she could have it, then she thought he was telling the truth. It was more important right now to get Helena and figure out what to do.

It took a little arguing to get Helena out of the water. Aggie understood the young woman's desire to rid herself of every vestige of her ordeal, but time was short. She finally impressed on Helena the importance of haste, of how the outlaws might come back.

Aggie surprised herself with her calmness. Her husband was lying dead just on the other side of the river there, and three of her husband's friends also were dead. There were dead outlaws behind her, and a wounded man sitting on a corpse. Death, pain, and suffering were all around her. Still, she was rather levelheaded, goading Helena Winslow into movement.

As they walked back toward Calhoun, Aggie explained to her friend about their benefactor. As Aggie suspected, Helena was not overly concerned that the man who had killed her husband was here again.

Calhoun was sitting in the same place. He had pulled another bandanna from his pocket and was holding it over the hole in his chest. He looked ghastly pale. The pain had returned.

The two women hurried over and knelt solicitously. "Let me see that," Aggie ordered.

"No time," Calhoun rasped.

"Like hell," Aggie snapped.

Calhoun moved the bandanna. Aggie ripped the shirt down so she could get a good look at the wound. She poked and prodded around it just a bit, impressed when Calhoun showed little reaction, though she knew it must be hurting him considerably.

"It ain't good," she said. "Ball's still in there. It'll have to come out."

"Later."

"What're we gonna do?" Helena asked. Her voice quavered with worry.

"First, get the hell out of here."

"How? Where?" Helena asked. Her fright was growing, and she was having trouble controlling it.

"Get hold of yourself, girl," Aggie snapped. She looked at Calhoun. "What do you suggest, Mister Calhoun?"

"You got horses?"

"Several."

"Can you both ride?"

"Yep. Astride, though that might shock some. We didn't get to a godforsaken place like Misfortune by ridin' sidesaddle."

Calhoun nodded. "Quickly, then, one of you saddle three horses. Use my saddle on one. I ain't about to ride that goddamn mule another step." He paused to catch his breath and let a wave of pain dwindle to manageable levels.

"The other of you can go 'round and pick up any usable supplies that's handy, then pack 'em on the mule. Use a second mule if you need it."

Aggie nodded. "Helena, get the supplies. I'll get the horses, then come help you."

"Make it fast, ladies," Calhoun said.

Aggie nodded again. She rose, feeling a little more sprightly now that she had a purpose.

"What're you gonna do, Mister Calhoun?" Helena asked.

"Take care of things," Calhoun said sourly. He hoped he had the strength. Right now he wasn't sure he did.

"What things?" Helena asked.

"Don't ask, child," Aggie said. She looked at Calhoun and smiled down wanly at him.

He looked up. He couldn't work up a smile in the best of circumstances; so he sure as hell couldn't find one now. "It ain't gonna be a good job, you know," he said quietly.

Aggie nodded. She had gone these past few minutes, since all the trouble started, without crying. She didn't want to start now, but she was on the verge of it.

"It's gonna have to be the river, if I can even manage that."

Aggie nodded again, tears falling. She could not stop them.

"What're you two talkin' about?" Helena asked in exasperation.

"Go about your business," Calhoun said. He struggled to rise. Aggie quickly reached out and grabbed his good arm. She hoisted him, surprising him with her strength. "Thanks," he said when he was on his feet.

He lurched down toward the river, moving slowly,

like an old man carrying a trunk of rocks on each shoulder. He limped, favoring the wounded leg. At the water's edge, he found that the two bodies that had been nearest this side had been swept away by the current. He stood looking out across the river, knowing he would never make it. Not in his condition. He turned and headed back toward the camp.

Aggie had saddled a horse for him first. He nodded thanks to the older woman, who was already saddling another. Pulling himself onto the big chestnut was an experience in agony, but he finally made it. However, it took several minutes for him to be able to move again.

Then he rode to the river and across. He slid off the horse, grabbed Armitage's body and hauled it up a little. Flames seared his chest, burning deep into his heart and lungs. He dropped the corpse and fell to his knees. Involuntary tears seeped out from behind his closed eyelids.

The agony subsided after a while, but still Calhoun knelt there. He wasn't so much afraid to move as it was not wanting to reawaken the spurts of pain. At last he gained the strength to stand. He wobbled to his new horse and got the coil of rope from his saddle horn.

Still moving slowly, he looped the rope over Armitage's ankles. Getting back on the horse was once again agonizing, but he made it. Dallying the rope around the saddle horn, he glanced across the river. Neither woman was looking this way. He rode into the river, dragging the corpse behind him on a short length of the rope. Once the current caught the body, Calhoun sliced the rope off.

He did the same with the other body. That was a little easier, since that body was partly in the river already. Then he rode back to the camp.

The women had made good progress, and were almost ready. Calhoun, not certain he would be able to get back on the horse again, stayed in the saddle, watching as Aggie and Helena packed some supplies on a second mule.

"One more load on another mule and we'll be ready, Mister Calhoun," Helena said. She stood, wiping stray hairs off her sweaty forehead. She was tall and graceful, with a slim neck and a nice figure. Her hair was the color of new honey.

"We'll take what we got now," Calhoun said. His voice was weak, but it still held command.

Helena began to argue. Aggie finished tying the last knot on the second mule. "Hush, child," she snapped. "And get on the horse."

CHAPTER

✴ 20 ✴

"Where do we go?" Aggie asked as she and Helena mounted. She seemed to have reconciled herself to all that had gone on.

"South," Calhoun said quietly. He was holding himself straight in the saddle only by dint of sheer will. He wanted nothing more than to fall to the ground; perhaps sleep for a week or two, until the pain went away. "There's a trail cuts through that niche in the rocks there across the river." He pointed.

Aggie nodded. Her seamed, old face was set in determination.

"You'll have to lead the way, Miz Aggie," he said. His words sounded distant to him; and weak.

"The trail clear?" Aggie asked. There was no worry evident in her voice.

"Fair. You'll have no trouble followin' it." He paused. "Reckon you ought to lead the pack mules, too. Miss Helena, you follow. I'll bring up the rear, and keep a watch on our back trail."

Calhoun stopped. It was as long a speech as he would normally make under any circumstances. In his depleted condition, it wore him out.

He gathered up his reserves and then looked around the barren mining camp. The canvas tents flapped in the breeze; flies buzzed around the bodies of the outlaws. It was altogether a forlorn place. There was nothing to keep any of them here; no reason whatever to linger.

"Let's ride," he announced.

"It's almost dark," Helena objected. She looked scared, and worried. Her pretty face was ashen, her pouty lips almost bloodless. "We going to ride through the night?"

"You can stay behind here, if you're of a mind to," Calhoun said sharply. He was in no mood to deal with someone with a weak will. He much preferred someone like Aggie Armitage right now. She had suffered greatly, including losing her husband less than half an hour ago. Yet she showed no signs of fear or worry. There was work to be done, and she was prepared to do it.

"But I . . . we . . ." Helena started.

"Hush up, child," Aggie snapped. "Snivelin' doesn't become you. Nor will it make our situation any better. Buck up and move, unless you'd rather have those men come back here for another shot at sportin' with you."

The older woman knew she was being brutal, but she had to be. If they were to survive, they could not sit here bickering and waffling. It was a time for action.

Aggie pulled her horse around and rode toward the river, cutting off further protest from her young friend.

Calhoun indicated with a slight jerk of his head that Helena should follow Aggie. Tight-lipped, Helena complied. As she moved by Calhoun, he said, "Everything'll be all right, ma'am."

She stopped and stared at him. Suddenly she felt heartened. If the old woman could make it after all that had happened to her; and if this man could be so determined despite such serious wounds, then she could hold up her end, too, she decided.

"I'd like to think it will, Mister Calhoun," Helena said quietly.

Calhoun nodded. "Just one thing, ma'am."

"Yes?" she asked, curious.

"Keep glancin' behind you as you're ridin'."

"Why?" she asked, surprised. It seemed such a strange request.

"I ain't so sure I won't fall off my horse somewhere," he confided. "I'll need you to keep an eye on me."

Helena smiled for the first time since Dunleavy's men had ridden into Misfortune. It was a dazzling smile, Calhoun thought, enough to excite any man, even one who was bleeding to death and losing strength by the minute. "I'll watch out for you," Helena promised. She was resolute.

Helena rode ahead, hurrying to catch up to Aggie, who was already edging into the water.

With a last look at the camp, Calhoun followed her. He blanked his mind to the pain that coursed through his body. He was fairly certain he would live — if he didn't lose too much blood. He glanced down at his chest. Just after he had returned from getting the bodies into the river, Aggie had ripped up one of her few spare dresses, and bandaged his chest. It seemed now that the flow of blood had been staunched.

The leg, too, seemed to have stopped bleeding, at least a lot. There might be some seepage. Still, Calhoun was weak and shaky from the blood he had lost, and from the long day of boredom followed by intensity. He did not look forward to traveling.

Calhoun noticed as he crossed the river that the bodies of Armitage and Mossback had been swept away. He was glad that Aggie had not had to see her husband's corpse; not after the way he had been killed.

On the far bank, Aggie was moving into the trees already. Her back was straight and lent an air of determination to their enterprise. Just across the river, Calhoun stopped and looked back. He pulled out his telescope and scanned the trees. As far as he could tell, Dunleavy, Fatback, and Peaches were nowhere around.

He sort of wished he had more strength. If he had, he could make an effort to cover up their tracks. If Dunleavy was planning to follow, Calhoun didn't want to make it any easier than necessary for the outlaws. He sighed. He could barely keep himself on his horse, let alone expend any extra energy on such things. He moved on.

It was dim and cool amid the thick pines and tall, spindly aspens, whose leaves whooshed in the face of the breeze. The sun went down soon, making it near pitch black in the forest. Aggie would stop at each glade they came to and wait in the moonlight. She would look back to see if Helena and Calhoun were behind her. When she saw that they were, she moved on again.

Helena glanced behind her frequently, worried about Calhoun. Most of the time she couldn't tell whether he was there or not, since it was so dark. She would stop occasionally and wait with bated breath until she heard him or until he almost ran into her before she moved on again. It was nerve-racking on her, but she kept silent. Neither of the others was complaining about the hardships.

The night seemed interminable, but finally dawn crept up on them. Aggie stopped in another clearing, with the sun hot despite just coming up. She waited for Helena, who stopped next to her, and then Calhoun.

The saddle tramp was moving slowly. He rode slackly, half bent over. The sudden brightness of the sun when he rode out of the trees caused him to look up, blinking. He didn't remember most of the ride through the night. It was almost as if he had suddenly come awake. Seeing Aggie and Helena waiting for him, he straightened.

"We need to eat," Aggie said sternly when Calhoun stopped near the two women.

"Ain't got time for that," he croaked. His voice didn't want to work right.

"Yes, we do." Despite her age and her latest tribulations, she seemed alert. Without waiting for a response, she eased out of the saddle. With her feet on the ground, she stretched. Then she rubbed her lower back and then buttocks. "Lordy, these old bones ain't used to these things no more," she said, trying to sound lighthearted.

Calhoun's lips moved. It could've been a smile.

Helena also dismounted. She had to hold onto the saddle, since her legs were wobbly. "Aggie's right," she said firmly.

"'Course I'm right," Aggie added with a raspy laugh. She grew serious. "Besides, Mister Calhoun, the animals need a rest. They've been hard used."

Calhoun cursed silently at himself. Aggie was right. He should have seen it for himself. He partially soothed his conscience by telling himself that his wounds had kept him preoccupied. He nodded. Still, he sat on his horse. He did not look forward to getting down. Doing so would be bad enough, but getting back on later would be the real test. With a sigh, he slid awkwardly to the ground.

He almost fell, grabbing the saddle to stop himself only at the last minute.

Helena made a move to go toward him, but Aggie stopped her. Helena looked at the older woman in surprise and anger, but then she realized why Aggie had done it. Calhoun would not want help at such a time. He needed to do this on his own.

"Get some firewood, child," Helena said quietly. "Then start a fire." As Helena hurried off, Aggie began unsaddling her horse. By the time Helena had gathered enough wood and had started a fire, all three horses were unsaddled and hobbled, grazing on the lush grass of the mountain meadow.

By that time, too, Calhoun was sitting, leaning back against a log. His legs were stretched out, his head was slumped onto his chest.

As Helena began cooking, Aggie went to Calhoun. "Now, Mister Calhoun," she said, "let's take another look at those wounds."

"They're all right," he protested, but only mildly.

"Sure they are." Aggie squatted down. "And I'm the queen of England." She smiled to take the sting out of the words. "Now, are you gonna let me look at 'em, or are you gonna make me arm wrestle you for the privilege?"

If Calhoun was a smiling type of man, he would have grinned. As it was, his lips twitched. He had a feeling that right now, she could probably outwrestle him easily. "Look all you like," he said.

Aggie bent close and pulled the bandage off Calhoun's chest. As she did, Calhoun was surprised to see that the older woman seemed somehow several years younger. Apparently the activity and having people need her had rejuvenated her. It was almost startling.

There was still little Aggie could do about Calhoun's wounds, but she cleaned them out with some water, made up a poultice of some sort and put it on before wrapping both in clean cloths. "There," she said, standing with the pile of bloody old bandages in her hands, "that ought to help you some." She looked worried. "We'll still need to get those bullets out of there."

Calhoun nodded. "It can wait."

"Till when?"

"Till we get somewhere safe."

"And where's that?" she asked.

"I got a place in mind." He hadn't thought too much of it before, really. He had thought at first of heading for Fortitude, but during that long ride through the night, he had decided against that. Dunleavy was almost certain to look for him there; might even be waiting there. Until he was recovered, Calhoun did not want to risk having to face down three men if he could help it.

There was more to it than that though, too, even if he didn't want to acknowledge it. He had set himself a job, and made a promise. He had said that he would bring the stolen money back to Fortitude. He was determined yet to do that—once he had finished the rest of his job. That would not be complete until Dunleavy, Peaches, and Fatback were dead.

"You gonna tell us where it is?" Aggie asked.

"Nope." He relented a little. "You'll see it when we get there."

"Why not Fortitude?" Aggie asked. She walked to the fire and tossed the old bandages into the flames, away from the food. Then she looked at him as she wiped off her hands.

He explained the former reason, if not the latter.

Aggie nodded, accepting the wisdom of it. She squatted beside the fire, her old skirt swirled around her in the grass. She poured a cup of coffee and brought it to him.

They ate speedily, though they made sure they got their fill. In his mind, Calhoun had set an hour as long enough for the horses to rest. It was a little more than that, but not much, when they finally got back on the trail. Getting back into the saddle was every bit as painful and difficult as Calhoun had thought it would be. But he showed little of the agony he felt.

They rode in the same formation as before. Calhoun figured that if Dunleavy's men were going to follow, now would be the time for it. He didn't really expect it, but one could never be entirely sure, especially with men like Dunleavy.

Late in the afternoon, Calhoun pulled up alongside Aggie and directed her onto a trail that cut southwest. She nodded and rode on. She was by far the oldest of the three, but she seemed to be the freshest. Calhoun's wounds were paining him considerably, and he was growing weaker by the hour. Helena did not complain, but Calhoun could see that she was exhausted.

Just after dark, Aggie pulled off the trail, into some brush. She had heard a brook bubbling there, and quickly found it. There were spaces between the trees, but no real clearing. Still, the grass ran right up to the water's edge and there was plenty of dry wood lying around.

Calhoun did not protest this time. He simply slid off the horse, wobbled off a few feet and plopped down heavily. He sat there watching the two women do the chores.

He ate heartily, the food giving him a little strength. Then he climbed into his bedroll and slept like the dead.

CHAPTER

✶ 21 ✶

C alhoun took over leading the way two mornings later. Sometime before noon, they entered a clearing from the small hill that overlooked the cabin. They splashed across the smaller stream, heading toward the rickety log building.

There were no signs that anyone had been at the cabin since Calhoun and Mary had left it. A few of the corral logs had fallen, and it looked like the one side of the cabin was sagging a little more than before. They were the only changes that Calhoun could see.

It was what he had hoped for. He had thought of this sometime during that first night. The cabin was more isolated than most places, even out in these wilds. And, since there seemed to be little placer gold in either of the streams right here, there would, he had suspected, be little interest in it. They probably would not be disturbed here. Calhoun figured it was the perfect spot to hole up and take the time to recover.

"What is this?" Helena asked as they edged down the slope toward the building.

"Just a cabin I knew of from days gone by," Calhoun said tightly.

Aggie looked at him sharply. From his look and the sound of his voice, she knew there was far more to it than that. She also knew this was not the time to question him about it. That time might never come; if it did, she would ask.

"Did you used to pan gold here, Mister Calhoun?" Helena asked innocently.

"No, ma'am," Calhoun said. He was trying not to be annoyed, but his wounds, and the tiredness that covered him like ants on a piece of meat made it difficult.

"Then what did . . . ?" Helena started to ask. She shut up when she saw the look of reproach Aggie gave her. She was surprised, but she figured she would ask Aggie about it later.

They rode to the cabin, stopped and dismounted. Helena headed for the door, but Aggie grabbed her and held her back. She nodded in Calhoun's direction.

Calhoun sucked in a deep breath to steady himself. He eased out a Dragoon and moved to the door. Flattening against the wall next to the door, he suddenly slapped a palm against the door, flapping it open.

After waiting a few seconds, he went in low and as fast as he could manage. The place was empty. He figured it was, since he had seen no sign of habitation, but he had wanted to make sure. He stood inside, wheezing, hands on his knees.

Finally he straightened and called, "Come on ahead."

Aggie and Helena came in. The older woman stood with her hands on her hips and surveyed the place with a critical eye. "Ain't the best place I've ever seen," she said, "but it's better than that flapping tent me and Leo had back in Misfortune." There was a slight hitch in her voice at the mention of her late husband, but she sloughed it off. She planned to do her grieving silently, like she had all along.

Helena looked at Calhoun. She was worried about him again. "You best set down, Mister Calhoun," she said solicitously. She went to him and took his arm.

"There's work to be done," he said. He wasn't sure how much he could do, but he thought he should make the effort.

"We'll see to it, Mister Calhoun," Aggie said. "Just like we've been doin'." She thought that might hurt him, so she hastily added, "Your job is to mend."

Calhoun nodded and reluctantly let Helena lead him to the nearest cot and help him to sit on it. As the two women went outside, he stretched out on the cot. He let his mind dwell for just a moment on what had transpired here on this very bed, but then he shut it out. He fell asleep.

He was rather befuddled when he awoke. He knew he was in the cabin near the two streams that ran down into Clear Creek. He wondered where Mary was, and why he was so wet.

Suddenly Aggie loomed over him, her seamed face even more creased with worry. Helena was there, too.

"You all right, Mister Calhoun?" Aggie asked.

"Reckon so." His brain was having trouble functioning yet. "Where's Mary?" he asked, worried.

"Mary?" Helena said in surprise. "Who's Mary?"

Aggie knelt next to the cot and dabbed at Calhoun's sweaty forehead with a cloth. "You remember where you are, Mister Calhoun?" she asked softly.

It slowly filtered back to him, all of it—Mary's death in Fortitude, the hunt for Mitch Dunleavy and his band of murderers, being wounded at Misfortune, the race to get here to the cabin. "Yes," he croaked. He struggled to get up.

Both women helped him, until he was finally sitting on the edge of the cot with his feet on the floor. His breathing was ragged, both from the effort and from the thoughts of Mary.

"How long was I out?" he finally asked, looking up first at Aggie, then Helena.

"Long enough," Aggie answered.

Calhoun could see bright sunlight through the cracks in the cabin walls. "All afternoon and night?" he asked.

Aggie nodded. "Hungry?"

"I expect."

Aggie hurried to get some food while Helena

helped Calhoun stand and then let him lean on her as he limped to the table. She eased him down in the seat. That allowed her to keep her hands on him as long as possible. She wondered if he noticed.

After he ate, he puffed on a cigarette and drank coffee.

As he did, Aggie said from the opposite side of the table, "We still got to get those bullets out of you, Mister Calhoun. It wouldn't do to let those wounds get too healed up and then have to cut into them again."

He nodded. He did not look forward to it, but it was better than the alternative. "You'll be able to do it?" he asked. He had few doubts.

"I've done so more times than I care to recall," Aggie said matter-of-factly.

Calhoun nodded again. "Best get out the whiskey, then," he said.

Aggie got a jug of whiskey from a shelf near the stove. She had had the foresight to bring all they had from Misfortune, knowing a good portion would be needed for this. Besides, after thirty-seven years of marriage, she knew that a man could use a few long drinks of whiskey from time to time just as a matter of course.

Calhoun could see no reason to put this off. He grabbed the jug and swallowed deeply. He kept on doing so until he was roaring, stinking drunk. Even more so than the last time he had been here, with Mary. He drank some more.

At some point, he vaguely remembered Helena helping him stagger to the cot. He could hear Aggie's voice telling him that it was better he do so now than try to have the two women cart him there after he had passed out.

He also remembered a sharp, stabbing pain in his chest, and he remembered the taste of the piece of pine one of the women had jammed between his teeth. Then there was blackness.

Calhoun grumbled around the cabin for three days before Aggie finally snapped at him, "You gonna be this cross the rest of your life, Mister Calhoun?" She had been pleasant and helpful all along, but now was tired of his peevishness.

He looked at her in some surprise, more at her tone than the words.

"Leave him alone, Aggie," Helena said defensively. "He's been hurt bad, and still has a heap of recoverin' to do."

"Pshaw," Aggie said angrily. "He's well on his way to recoverin'. Ain't you, Mister Calhoun?"

Calhoun thought about that a little. It was true. It had been more than a week since Aggie had cut the bullets out of him. He had slept drunkenly the rest of the day and most of the night. He awoke in agony, though he tried to hide it. Aggie had sensed it, and came and dosed him with more whiskey until he was asleep again.

She kept dosing him with alcohol for several days, during which time he slipped in and out of consciousness. The pain would come and go. He never knew that he had spent some time in delirium, and that both Aggie and Helena had nursed him day and night, always with him to change poultices, wipe the sweat of fever off his body, or to force more whiskey down his throat.

When he had finally awoke for real, he was in a bearish mood. He did not like being helpless around others, particularly women. He was embarrassed by what he saw as his weakness then, and did not know how to cope with it. Hence, his sour attitude.

Calhoun took a deep breath. "Yes, ma'am, you're right," he said. He had acted that way long enough. It was time to stop it. Wade Calhoun was not, even under the best of circumstances, a sociable man, but he could get along with people when the need arose.

Like now. Besides, he could see no reason for treating Aggie and Helena poorly. Not after having to put up with all they had, and not after all the help they had given him. They certainly owed him nothing and deserved better treatment than he had given them.

He did not fully recover overnight, of course, but he seemed to get a little better every day. After two more weeks—ones in which he ate heartily and often—he began venturing outside. By the end of the fourth week since awakening, he was practicing with his pistols, trying to get back his shooting eye. It had never really left him, but he knew that a man had to keep sharp at such things. Especially since he still had a job to complete.

The week after that, he even saddled his new chestnut mare and rode out a little ways. Helena had fretted about it, thinking that perhaps he would fall off his horse out there and die, leaving her and Aggie alone and defenseless.

Calhoun had gone anyway. She had no hold on him, no claim to him. He was not one to be tied down by such things anyway. He returned with a deer carcass, and they ate well on fresh venison that night and for two days afterward, until the meat had gone rancid.

Then he rode out hunting again, and was as successful as the last time. Helena had given him a reproving look when he had left the cabin, but she said nothing.

That night, though, after Aggie had gone to bed, Helena scolded him quietly for his solitary excursions.

"I'm near recovered," he told her flatly, "and I need to do such things." He was not fond of explaining himself to anyone.

"But what if somethin' was to happen to you?" she asked, staring at him with wide, luminous eyes.

"You and Aggie'd be on your own," Calhoun said with a shrug. "Aggie's a smart and tough old woman. She'd get you and her somewhere, if it was necessary."

"But . . ."

Calhoun suddenly realized that there was more to what Helena was telling him than what she was saying. He didn't want to make any incorrect assumptions, though. "Say what you mean, Miss Helena," he urged.

She looked down at her hands, which wriggled on the table. "I'd miss you somethin' awful, Mister Calhoun," she said quietly.

"Even though I'm the one killed your husband not so long ago?" he asked harshly.

"Yes." She looked into his eyes. Hers were wide, but there were no tears to be seen. After a moment, she said, "Chris Winslow wasn't an easy man to live with. In fact, he was a skunk." She looked down at her hands again for a few moments, before gazing back at him. "He was mean and rough. He beat me and . . ." She bit her full lower lip, as if trying through the pain to stem the tears that were threatening.

She sucked in a ragged breath and looked at Calhoun, somewhat defiantly. "Before we come to Misfortune, he would pass me around to his cronies—for some money of course—in other minin' camps."

Calhoun winced inwardly. He never could understand how or why men would do such things to women they supposedly cared for.

"I was," Helena went on after a moment, "rather relieved when you killed him, Mister Calhoun," she said matter-of-factly. She smiled regretfully.

"Of course, what happened later wasn't much better than what I had with Chris. The three who were left in Misfortune—excludin' Mister Armitage, of course—bid over me. Enos Pennrose won out, and took me to his tent." She sighed. "He wasn't as mean as Chris, but . . . well, he wasn't much of a man, neither." She flushed.

"You have my sympathies, ma'am," Calhoun said kindly but noncommittally.

Helena nodded. "And what sort of man are you, Mister Calhoun?" she asked boldly.

Calhoun shrugged, but he felt a stirring of excitement. He was nearly recovered from his wounds, but he had yet to fully prove himself in all ways.

"I'd say a pretty good one," Helena added. She looked at him speculatively. She stood, not believing she was being quite so brazen, and walked around the table toward him.

She found out that night that she was right. Calhoun learned, too, that the wounds had had no lasting effect on him.

CHAPTER

✳ 22 ✳

"What's your plan, Mister Calhoun?" Aggie asked after breakfast. It had been another two weeks or so, and Calhoun seemed to be about fully recovered.

"Well," he said after a moment's thought and another sip of coffee, "reckon I'll take you two down to Fortitude."

"And then?"

"Then you'll be on your own."

"And what about you?" Helena asked. Her voice caught a little, and she hoped no one noticed. She and Calhoun had spent the past two weeks—ever since that first night—together, and she had high hopes that they would have a future together. She thought Calhoun a fine man, much better than her late husband and the man she had been taken by afterward.

Calhoun shrugged. "I've got business to finish."

"With that . . . that . . . ?" Helena started. She could not finish it.

"Mitch Dunleavy's his name," Calhoun said.

"Why're you so all fired set on findin' this Dunleavy feller?" Aggie asked shrewdly. "It can't be what he done over in Misfortune. The men he and his cronies killed there meant nothing, less than nothin' to you. Includin' my husband." There was a note of sadness at the last. While she might not grieve publicly, she still missed him terribly. They had been together far too long and had had a good enough life not to.

She paused a minute, then said, "Indeed, Mister Calhoun, you had some reason to be glad seein' them shot down."

"Expect I did." He shrugged again and stubbed out his cigarette on the table. He didn't really owe the two women an account, but they had suffered mightily, and Calhoun thought that some sort of explanation was deserved.

Without frills or inflection, he sketched out what had happened to Mary down in Fortitude. He didn't delve into their relationship very much; just enough that the women would understand Calhoun's desire for revenge.

He also explained, briefly, that he had promised to find Dunleavy, get the money that was stolen, and return it to the bank at Fortitude.

Aggie could understand that honor, though her eyes and ears perked up at the thought of ten thousand dollars in gold. She could be set up for life, she thought, and not have to end up marrying some other footloose miner. Such would be her fate if she got to Fortitude, though with the six hundred dollars in gold Calhoun had given back, plus the gold the miners had accumulated in Misfortune, she wasn't destitute.

Still, there was no place for an old woman alone out here, and unless she could use the money to some good for herself, she would end up having to marry the first miner who came along and made the best offer.

Helena, she figured, would have it somewhat easier. Helena's choices also were limited, but being young and quite attractive, she would have her pick of men.

Of course, Aggie could see that Helena had already picked the man she wanted. Trouble was, Aggie could also see that Calhoun did not want to be picked, by Helena or anyone else. She suspected there was more to this man's story than the woman he had mentioned as the one who was killed in Fortitude. It was not her place to pry, though she had the feeling that she would have to provide some comfort for Helena before long.

"Why don't you just take us with you?" Helena asked. She wanted to stay with Calhoun, knowing that if he left her someplace, he might never return. The thought of the money had also struck her. She figured she and Calhoun could have quite a good life with ten thousand dollars.

"No," Calhoun said flatly. He had enjoyed his time with Helena, and would miss it a little when it ended. Helena Winslow was an attractive and exciting young woman, but Calhoun had no plans to settle down with her. He had come close to thinking about such a thing with Mary, only to have her be killed. He would not go through that again.

"Why?" Helena asked. Her full lower lip trembled.

"It'd put you in too much danger," he said. It was true, and he hoped it would suffice for her, since Calhoun did not want to explain to her that they had no future together.

Helena could not argue with that, though she wanted to. She kept silent, but she folded her arms over her breasts and sulked.

"When're you fixin' to leave, Mister Calhoun?" Aggie asked. Dreams of the gold still danced in her head, but she was a practical woman, too. She still would like to get her hands on that money, though it seemed unlikely. Still, things could change rapidly out here. First things first.

"Tomorrow. Maybe the next day, if you need a little more time to get ready."

"We'll start now," Aggie said.

Calhoun nodded. He stood and yawned. He might be fully recovered, but he knew his strength still had a ways to go before being back to what it had been. "I'll be back after a spell," he said. "We could use more meat."

While that was true enough, Calhoun also wanted

to be alone for a while. He enjoyed his time with Helena, and he enjoyed gabbing with old Aggie. He valued his time alone, though. He was a solitary man by nature, especially since he had lost Lisbeth, and he had spent entirely too much time in the company of others lately.

He grabbed his saddle and headed out to the corral. The day was hot and muggy. The constant breeze kicked up puffs of dust, and insects buzzed and hummed. Calhoun saddled the chestnut and rode out.

Calhoun stopped just within the screen of trees and looked down the rocky slope at the cabin, and the cliff beyond. Stopping in the cover of the foliage was a habit he had picked up, an instinctive move that he didn't even realize he was doing most of the time.

"Damn," he cursed, looking at the scene. Three saddled horses were tied to the rails of the corral. Calhoun had seen those three horses before. It was almost two months ago, in the mining camp the tin panners had called Misfortune.

Sitting there, watching, Calhoun realized he should not have been surprised. Had he thought about it, he would have known it was only a matter of time before Dunleavy and his two remaining cronies found him. After all, he had found Dunleavy's men the first time, and would have done so again.

What did surprise him was that Dunleavy had not picked up more men along the way somewhere. There was no shortage of cutthroats and thieves in the mountains.

Calhoun shoved the deer carcass that was lying across his saddle in front of him onto the ground. He dismounted and tied the chestnut to a tree branch. He pulled his telescope out of his saddlebags, and squatted behind a bush. He watched and waited.

He steeled himself to what he supposed was happening inside the rickety cabin. If Dunleavy, Fatback, and Peaches had been there more than a few minutes, the women, or at least Helena, would've been assaulted already. There was a possibility that the outlaws had left the women alone, preferring to wait instead to kill him before enjoying themselves unhampered with the women. Calhoun could only hope that was so, though he doubted it.

It was much harder for Calhoun to steel himself against a new wave of self-recrimination. Though he would never be able to do so where Lisbeth was concerned, he had finally managed to bring himself to where he could live with the fact that he had brought about Mary's death. Now this.

He was as recovered as he was going to get; had been for a week or more. Yet he had lingered on here, enjoying his intimacy with Helena; not wanting to end the comfortable existence. Even this morning, when

Aggie had questioned him about it, he had put off leaving for another day or two. Had he had the gumption to leave when he should have, the women would be in Fortitude, and not being endangered by Dunleavy's pack of wolves.

With a sigh of annoyance at his self-loathing, he rolled and lit a cigarette, cupping the match against the breeze. Since the door was the only way to see out of the cabin, and it was closed, he was not worried about being spotted.

After he finished the smoke, he started thinking about what to do. That was a vexatious problem. He could just ride on down there and hope to surprise them, but that would more than likely be fatal. Even if the three outlaws weren't watching every minute, someone was bound to look outside occasionally, and there was too much open ground between here and the cabin to make it safely. Unless he galloped, in which case the noise would alert those inside.

He could wait till dark, which might be the safest, at least for him. But in that case, the women might be ravaged, or even killed. He had been responsible for enough women being killed; he did not want to allow any more, if he could help it.

Sneaking down to the cabin would be hard, but possible. Having the cabin backed up against the cliff like it was and having so much open ground in front limited his possible approaches to two sides. There were not enough trees on either side to make it comfortable. On the northern side was the corral, which meant he would have to get past not only his animals but the ones of the outlaws. Any one of them might give away his presence.

He could cut the outlaws' horses loose and send them running, which might draw them out. On the other hand, it was more likely that when they realized their horses were loose that he would be around, and close. That would make them stay inside the cabin, using the women for hostages. Such a thing would never do.

One of the streams passed on the south side. It was not a big stream, but it was cold and flowed with a strong current. Getting across it would be the trickiest part.

He waited a little longer, considering every possibility. He had already decided that he could not wait much longer, leaving the women at risk. He had to go down there and try to do something. He realized that there was only one real option—crossing the stream and coming up on the south side of the cabin. One advantage he would have was that there were no windows in the cabin. Any side he came up on, except the front, would be a blind side for those inside.

Calhoun stood and backed up. He dropped the telescope into his saddlebags. Quickly he tied a rope around the deer carcass and hoisted it over a high tree limb. That would keep it away from most scavengers, and the bigger carnivores. He and the women would still have to eat after he had taken care of Dun-leavy and the two others.

As he rode back through the trees, he thought about his assault. He had no idea of what he would do when he got to the cabin. He would let that sort itself out when he got there. First he had to make it that far.

He worked around through the trees, down toward where the smaller stream emptied into the larger. He crossed over into the trees that ran along the larger stream, and then followed the trees along the stream west, almost to the cliff.

At last he dismounted and tied the chestnut to a tree again. He sat and took off his spurs. After dropping them into his saddlebags, he pulled one of the big Colt Walkers from the saddle holster. He thought about taking the scattergun, but realized it probably would do him little good. Firing off that 10-gauge shotgun in the cabin likely would harm the woman as well as the outlaws. With a deep breath, and the Walker in his right fist, he headed out of the trees.

The knee-deep water in the stream was bitter cold, despite the heat of the day. Calhoun ignored its icy bite as best he could as he waded across. He was not worried about noise, seeing as how the stream bubbled loudly over rocks. He made it to the far banks and sloshed hurriedly to the cabin.

He was breathing rather heavily as he pressed against the wall. He was not in as good a shape as he had thought, he realized. It took some minutes before his breathing was back to normal. He turned and pressed his eye to one of the many cracks in the log wall.

It was difficult to see, what with the sun so bright outside and the dimness of the cabin's interior. Most of his eyesight also was restricted by the cook stove and the cabinets and such that made the south side of the abode into something of a kitchen.

He moved silently toward the corner of the cabin. Stopping, he peered around. As far as he could tell, the door was still closed, and there was no one outside.

Suddenly a bullet tore out a chunk of the cabin an inch from his head.

"Shit," Calhoun breathed. He did not hesitate to decide what was going on. He simply whirled and ran for the stream, going full out. He splashed across the water and headed at a run into the trees.

Without stopping, he flung himself up into the saddle. He ripped the reins from the branch, and lashed the horse with the ends. The animal bolted down the trail on which they had come. Calhoun put his head down, trying to keep from being lashed by branches and such as the horse thundered along.

All the while, he managed to keep his mind off the disgust he felt with himself. Off the fact that he had been so complacent as to not bother checking all over to see if the outlaws had left someone outside to wait for him.

He had assumed it was their arrogance that led them to leave their horses in plain sight, not as a trap for him. His anger at himself grew considerably.

CHAPTER
* 23 *

About the time he hit the spot where he had left the deer carcass, Calhoun slowed, and then stopped. He was not about to make the same mistake twice. He had underestimated the enemy before, and it had almost been fatal.

Besides, he had to think things through. It was, he realized, quite possible that the women were dead and all three outlaws posted in the trees, waiting for him. He did not think that likely, though. First, Dunleavy would want to keep at least Helena alive, both for sporting and as a hostage as a last resort. In addition, if they were all waiting in the trees to ambush him, they would be spread out in an arc based on the front of the cabin. Were that the case, Calhoun would have seen at least one of them already.

It was most likely that Dunleavy and one of his cronies were inside with the women. Perhaps sporting with them, perhaps just keeping an eye on them until Calhoun was dispatched.

Calhoun worried a little about the gunshot. Surely Dunleavy and whoever else was inside with him would be curious as to whether their companion had gotten him. As far as Calhoun could tell, no one had poked his head outside to check. Nor had there been any shouted communications about it. He guessed that those inside must figure their friend had either missed and was waiting for another shot, or else he would be walking into the cabin soon. That would have the men in the cabin extra alert.

Calhoun also figured that would make his getting in to rescue the women all the more difficult. However, that would have to wait. First there was some unfinished business out here on the tree-covered hillside.

Calhoun tied off the horse, took his telescope and moved toward the rim of trees. Just inside it, he scanned the hillside to the north, trying to spot the outlaw. He had never seen where the shot had come from, but he had a rough idea. Still, he was not foolish enough to think that the outlaw, having possibly missed a shot at him, would just sit.

He saw nothing, but he knew that meant little. The rifleman was still out there somewhere. He would just have to find him. Calhoun mounted the chestnut and rode on a little more, working carefully through the trees and brush. Once more he stopped and dismounted, tying the horse. Then he went forward on foot.

Calhoun took his time. He figured that if those in the cabin were concerned about their companion outside, they would have checked by now. He also figured they were still down in the cabin, waiting. They would be more alert, but at the same time, since they knew Calhoun was around now, they most likely would be leaving the women alone.

Calhoun stalked silently through the forest, ignoring the time, and the sweat, and the heat, and insects. He stopped every several feet and waited, stock-still, holding his breath for a few minutes while he listened for any sound that would give the enemy away. His eyes scanned the trees for anything out of place.

He had no idea how long it took, but he finally spotted something that did not seem to belong in the forest. He couldn't tell what it was, but he thought it a piece of cloth, possibly a shirt. He nodded and moved on.

Calhoun's face revealed none of the revulsion he felt for himself when, a few moments later, he felt a pistol barrel jammed into his lower back, and heard a nasally voice saying, "'Bout time you showed up. I was plumb tired of waitin' on ya."

"That you, Peaches?" he asked bitterly, guessing.

"Yep. Now move yer ass." He prodded Calhoun's back none too gently.

"Where?" as Calhoun stepped off.

"Where in hell you think? Dunleavy said if I could take you alive, I should bring ya into the cabin."

"Then why'd you try'n take my head off when I was down by the cabin?"

"Wasn't. Wanted ya to come lookin' fer me like ya done. Now move."

A moment later they came upon the sign that had attracted Calhoun's attention. It was indeed a piece of cloth—Peaches's shirt. Calhoun felt like slitting his own throat. Fooled by a man's shirt hanging on a bush.

"Stop," Peaches commanded. Calhoun did. "Now ease out them pistols and drop 'em behind ya. Then the knife on your belt and that big pig sticker hanging under your arm."

Calhoun slowly did what he was told. "Why don't you just kill me now?" he asked.

"Reckon Mitch'd prefer doin' it himself, seein's how ya caused him so much trouble."

Out of the corner of his eye, Calhoun saw Peaches's wrinkled hand reach out and take the shirt. He held his breath. He hoped the outlaw was arrogant enough to stop and put it on. He might have a chance to take him; it might be his only chance. He harbored no illusions about being taken, virtually unarmed into that cabin with three killers.

The muzzle of the pistol left his back, and Calhoun was sure now that Peaches was putting his shirt on. Calhoun figured it was now or never. There was the probability that he would die in the next few moments, but he could not let himself be taken unarmed into that cabin. Besides, he thought bitterly, as foolish as he had acted since discovering the outlaws at the cabin, he deserved to die.

He whirled. In less time it took to blink, his eyes drank in the scene, and he reacted.

Peaches was standing there, pistol in an awkward position after he had transferred it to the other hand to be able to pull on his left sleeve.

Calhoun's left hand darted forward and latched on to the pistol, the lower part of his index finger stuffed into the space between hammer and cap. His right snapped a short, sharp punch to Peaches's face.

The outlaw's head jerked back, and his finger tightened on the trigger. The hammer snapped down hard on Calhoun's finger. He winced and yanked the pistol free. With the Colt clamped onto his left hand, Calhoun hammered several more punches on Peaches's head and face.

Peaches staggered back, coming up against a tree. At his age, his reflexes had slowed some, but he was a wily man, one who had survived many a year in cutthroat doings. He ducked, and Calhoun's next punch only grazed the side of his head before bouncing off the tree trunk.

Peaches tried kicking Calhoun in the groin. Calhoun managed to turn it aside, but the attempt angered him even more. He slammed a hard fist into Peaches's ribs, cracking some.

The outlaw groaned and sagged.

Calhoun suddenly felt better about himself. He had acted the fool, but he laid that to the fact that he had been wounded and out of commission for long enough that his abilities had rusted some. Now, however, he felt he was back to his normal self.

"You made one big goddamn mistake when you killed that woman down in Fortitude," he said, words raspy with rage.

"That Injin bitch?" Peaches commented. His voice was ragged with pain.

Calhoun kept his temper in check. Calmly, he pulled the hammer back on Peaches's Colt and unclamped it from his hand. He worked the index finger, grateful that it was not broken, though it would be sore and swollen for a while. He eased down the revolver's hammer.

"Yeah, that Injin bitch," he said.

Peaches did not like the look in Calhoun's eyes, not one bit. "She killed Pace," he said, his nasal whine irritating Calhoun.

"Too bad she didn't kill all you scum."

"What're you gonna do?" Peaches asked, clutching his cracked ribs.

"What the hell you think?" Calhoun responded sarcastically. He hefted Peaches's Colt a moment, then suddenly stepped up and began lashing the outlaw's head with it. He felt the heat rise in him as pictures of Mary's bloody body burned into his mind.

Something, but he was not sure what, finally made him end the pistol-whipping. He stepped back and looked down at the bloody heap. Peaches's head was pulp, almost unrecognizable, and his wrinkled chest was covered with blood.

Calhoun shrugged and turned away. He tossed Peaches's weapon into the brush and retrieved his own. Then he marched down toward the cabin. He came up from the side, but he did not hide. If the horses gave him away, he figured, so be it. There was no more time for him to be wary.

He moved swiftly, with his usual calm assurance. At the cabin wall, he did as before, and peered through the cracks in the logs. He had trouble seeing, but he spotted Helena and Aggie on the nearest cot, huddled together. Aggie had her arm around the younger woman, as if protecting her. He could not see their faces, but both seemed scared, though unharmed.

He caught the dim outlines of the aptly named Fatback pacing the cabin. Dunleavy sat at the table.

"Where the hell is he?" Calhoun heard Fatback say. "Damn, Peaches shoulda got that sombitch by now."

"Just relax. Peaches knows what he's doin'."

"Ought to've let me stay out there and get him," Fatback growled.

"Hell, you couldn't hit one of these cabin walls from inside here," Dunleavy snapped.

"You suppose he got him with that shot we heard a while back?"

"He was sure of it, he'd be back here by now. Since he ain't, I figure he missed. 'Course, you can go on outside and check, if you're of a mind to."

"What I'm of a mind to," Fatback said with a disgusting, phlegmy laugh, "is sportin' with that little bitch back there."

"You'll wait till business is taken care of," Dunleavy said angrily. "And then you'll wait your turn."

"How come I'm always last with such things, damn it?" His blubber jiggled with agitation.

"Because, you fat slob," Dunleavy snarled, standing to glare at Fatback, "once you throw your lard-filled carcass on a woman, she's either unconscious or of no use to the rest of us." He sat back down. Calhoun could see that his back was tense. He drank deeply from a mug that Calhoun figured contained whiskey.

Fatback took up his pacing again.

Calhoun almost smiled. He had made his mind up. Quickly he checked the loads in both Dragoons. It wouldn't do to have them misfire at a critical time because a cap had fallen off or the powder had gotten damp.

All seemed well with them. With a Colt in each hand, he slid around the corner of the building. Silently but boldly he headed toward the cabin door. When he got there, he stopped, and leaned forward a little.

There was a two-inch gap between the door and the jamb. He placed an eye to it and surveyed the scene. It was as before.

Calhoun put the Dragoon on his right hand back in the holster. Very gently, very carefully, he pulled the rawhide cord to the latch. The latch moved up, Calhoun could see through the crack. He kept pulling ever so softly. Finally the latch slipped with a soft click.

Inside, Fatback paused in his pacing. "What was that?" he asked, glancing around blankly, like a whale wondering how he had gotten stranded on shore.

Calhoun held his breath.

"What was what?" Dunleavy mumbled.

Fatback shrugged his ponderous shoulders. "Nothin', I guess." He returned to his lumbering pacing.

Calhoun pulled the other Dragoon in his right hand again. Once more he pressed his eye to the gap in the doorway. He watched, waiting until Fatback's movement turned his back to the door.

Suddenly Calhoun kicked the door open and lunged inside.

CHAPTER
* 24 *

Three things happened simultaneously as the cabin door crashed open: Helena and Aggie screamed, their voices echoing in the room; Fatback whirled with a speed that was amazing in so ponderous a man; and Dunleavy half stood and turned toward the door.

Calhoun took in the scene with a single glance. He knew that Fatback, obese as he was, was the more dangerous right now. Dunleavy was hampered from drawing a pistol by the table, and by still being sideways to Calhoun. But Fatback was facing him, and already hauling out a big Remington in a meaty fist.

Three balls from one of Calhoun's Dragoons hammered Fatback in the chest. Each blow shoved the corpulent man back a step or two, until the third drove him hard against the wall. His blubbery body, light already beginning to fade from the eyes, slid down the wall, leaving trails of blood along the rough logs. He landed on his plump buttocks. He looked almost comical as he stared with dying eyes at Calhoun, wondering just what had happened.

Fatback made a last effort to raise the Remington, but it was too heavy for him. He expired with a faintly obscene sigh.

Calhoun was not watching him, though. He knew the damage he had wrought to the fat man was fatal, and he swung toward Dunleavy. Rage colored his vision red, and he ached to pull the trigger. Still, he hesitated.

"Sit your ass down and put your hands flat on the table," he hissed.

Dunleavy delayed an instant, and Calhoun let a slug fly. The ball clipped Dunleavy's left ear. Dunleavy's eyes widened with the pain. He was startled that Calhoun had done it. He began to sweat, as he plopped quickly down into the chair again.

"Where's the money?" Calhoun asked harshly, moving a few steps closer.

"What money?" Dunleavy responded, trying to look innocent.

Calhoun fired the final shot from the one Dragoon, taking off the top half of Dunleavy's other ear. Calhoun slid that empty Dragoon into the holster and shifted the other pistol to his right hand.

Dunleavy was shocked, and in considerable pain. Both ears stung. He wanted to touch them, to see what the damage was, but he knew that even the slightest movement would bring only more trouble for him.

"I ain't gonna ask you but one more time, boy. Where's the money?"

Dunleavy licked his lips. He could feel the sweat rolling down his face. He was used to creating fear, not feeling it. "Most of it's gone," he offered.

"Bullshit," Calhoun snapped.

"Wc spent it," Dunleavy protested.

"Like hell." Calhoun reached up and scratched the side of his head with the pistol barrel and sighed. He hated it when people tried to play him for a fool. "There ain't no place in these mountains you could've spent that much money, except Fortitude, and you sure as hell weren't gonna go back there to blow it."

"We hauled ass to California. Blew it all in Sacramento."

"You ain't had time."

"It's been more'n two months." Dunleavy was beginning to feel a little more relaxed. With the calmness he should be able to plot an escape from this madman.

"I know," Calhoun said quietly. He remembered most of it—the pain, the loss, the days of delirium, the race for life. "Trouble is, I expect you was lookin' for me most of that time." His face hardened.

Dunleavy's skin tightened as fear reared its head anew.

"Now, where's the money?"

Dunleavy hesitated. He knew that there would be no escape, unless he could kill Calhoun. That would be damn near impossible, he figured, but he would have to give it a try.

It was too late, though. The delay was costly. Calhoun was of no mood to wait. He simply fired again, putting a bullet through Dunleavy's right bicep. The bone snapped, and blood flowed. Dunleavy hissed as he sucked a quick breath through his teeth.

"Well?" Calhoun asked.

"I . . . I . . ." His eyes widened and fear gripped his bowels as he saw Calhoun's finger tighten on the trigger. "Wai . . ." he screeched, partly in fear, partly from the newest blast of pain as his left arm was rendered useless from a bullet.

Dunleavy sat, breathing heavily. The agony was intense; he had never felt anything like this before. Through pain-clouded eyes, he looked at Calhoun, and saw a man as hard and resolute as he himself usually was.

"Who the hell are you?" he asked, voice cracking with pain.

"Name's Wade Calhoun."

"Why . . . ?" Dunleavy asked, amazed. He had never seen this man before the encounter in Misfortune.

"The robbery in Fortitude."

"What's that to you?" Dunleavy asked in wonder. "You don't look like no tin pan to me. You couldn't've lost no money from that."

Dunleavy was shocked at the look of hatred and rage on Calhoun's face. "You ought to pay more attention to folks you kill," Calhoun said, his voice grating and harsh as a rockslide.

"Who?"

"Mary White Feather Crowley."

Dunleavy looked blankly through his pain. "Who's she?" he asked dumbly.

"Half-breed woman standing with some horses and mules in Fortitude that day. You and your cronies gunned her down."

The light of recognition switched on in Dunleavy's eyes. He nodded, careful not to move his damaged arms, lest he sent a new wave of pain racing through him. "I remember," he said carefully.

He tried to look apologetic, while at the same time build a bit of manly camaraderie. "But she was takin' potshots at us. Hell, she even took out Pace, one of my best men." Dunleavy shrugged, then gasped with pain. When he settled down again, he added, "Hell, what was we supposed to do, just let her sit there and send the rest of us cross the divide?"

"Would've saved a heap of others considerable trouble," Calhoun growled. "Now, where's that money?"

"Mind if I ask a question first?" Dunleavy requested, a note of urgency in his voice.

Calhoun shrugged.

"What're you gonna do with me?"

"Haul you back to Fortitude," Calhoun said glibly. "I suspect those folks could do with a necktie party."

Dunleavy nodded. He was fairly certain Calhoun was lying, but he had to take the slight chance that Calhoun was telling the truth. If he continued to be recalcitrant, he was sure that Calhoun would kill him in an instant. If he told where the gold was, Calhoun might keep him alive, at least for a while. With each minute of life, there might come the possibility of escape. The possibility was slim, granted, but it was better than no chance at all.

He sighed. "Me, Fatback, and Peaches—you took care of Peaches, I assume?" he suddenly asked.

Calhoun nodded.

Dunleavy shook his head. His hopes were fading, but he still retained a little. "We buried it down the trail a ways on the way here."

"Where?"

"Southwest, maybe two miles. There's a giant split rock off the trail to the south. Ten yards east, we cached it under a hackberry."

Calhoun nodded again. "Stand," he ordered. When Dunleavy had done so, Calhoun moved up and pulled the man's guns and knives out and dropped them on the table. "Miz Aggie," he said, "would you clean and bind his wounds, please." He watched as Aggie did as she was told.

Through it all, Dunleavy's hope began to build

again. Calhoun would not go through this much trouble if he was simply going to kill him.

Calhoun put his pistol away, and then tied Dunleavy to the chair. He went outside, returning less than ten minutes later. He untied Dunleavy from the chair, but bound his hands together. "Let's go," he said harshly.

"Where?"

"Fetch the gold."

Dunleavy felt a rush of relief that he had told the truth. He still figured that Calhoun would keep him alive for a while now.

The gold was where Dunleavy had said it was. The digging for it did not improve Calhoun's disposition any, and he regretted a little having disabled Dunleavy. He should have made the outlaw do the work. Retrieving the gold helped some, though.

As soon as he had the bags of gold dust, nuggets, and coins out on the ground, he paused for a drink of water and to wipe his sweating face.

At last he turned toward Dunleavy. The outlaw was in pain, that much was evident, but he still retained something of a smug look about him. Anger flooded Calhoun again as he walked toward Dunleavy. He roughly untied the outlaw's hands. "Move," he ordered.

The arrogance dropped from Dunleavy's face like

a stone. "Where?" he asked, mouth suddenly as dry as the Mojave Desert.

Calhoun pointed to the shallow hole.

Dunleavy shook his head. There was nothing Calhoun could do to him now to make him cooperate in his own death.

Calhoun grabbed the outlaw by the shirt and gave him a mighty shove. Dunleavy stumbled toward the hole. He could not stop, as his foot hit the crumbling dirt of the rim. He fell in, throwing out his arms to break his fall. He screamed when his shattered limbs collapsed under his weight.

"Get up," Calhoun ordered.

Dunleavy was in too much agony to answer. Calhoun waited a few minutes, then repeated his order.

Dunleavy looked up over his shoulder. His eyes were gray and dull. He shook his head. He managed to turn over onto his back. "Go ahead and kill me," he said listlessly.

Calhoun shrugged and shot Dunleavy in the stomach. He walked over and squatted alongside the outlaw. "After what you done, you deserve worse'n this," Calhoun said roughly.

"Kill me, you chicken-hearted son of a bitch," Dunleavy whispered, clutching his guts.

Calhoun almost smiled as he stood. Being gut shot was a bad enough way to die, he figured. It took a while, and was very painful. He thought it at least somewhat fitting, considering all the pain and grief

Dunleavy and his band of cutthroats had caused. Still, it was too good for Dunleavy.

Calhoun grabbed the shovel and began tossing dirt over the outlaw, who screeched and screamed. There was little Dunleavy could do. He tried to scrabble out of the hole, but each shovelful of dirt knocked him back. Finally he was covered except for his face.

Calhoun tossed the shovel away, turned, and began to load the money on Dunleavy's horse. It was one hell of a lot of money, he thought. Enough to set a man up for life. He sighed. The money was not his. More importantly, though, he had given his word to bring it back.

Finally he mounted his chestnut. "*Adios,*" Calhoun said softly. He rode back to the cabin.

When Calhoun entered the crude building, the two women were trying to get about their chores while ignoring the blubbery body of Fatback laying half on the floor, half against the wall.

"Where's . . . ?" Helena asked. She hated Dunleavy almost as much as Calhoun did, and wanted him dead. She surely hoped Calhoun hadn't let the outlaw go just because he had returned the gold.

"He met with an accident," Calhoun said sourly.

"Oh," Helena said. She was relieved.

Calhoun grabbed a hold of Fatback's belt buckle. With a considerable effort, he dragged the corpse outside. He tied a rope around the legs and, after dallying the other end of the rope to his saddle, dragged it off into the woods and dropped it.

He went back, unsaddled and curried his horse, then unloaded the gold, stacking it against the side of the building.

Helena and Aggie watched the latter. "That's a heap of cash there, Mister Calhoun," Aggie said quietly.

"Yes'm."

"Nobody'd ever have to know was we to just head north or east, or anywhere else."

Helena was a little shocked, but then she realized the possibilities of it. "No one'd be the wiser, that's for sure," she interjected.

"I would," Calhoun said simply.

The two women glared at him for a few moments. Then Aggie grinned. "I reckon that gold'd do nothin' more than get me in trouble," she said with a chuckle. "Why, what would an old lady like me do with that much money anyway?"

"You ain't so old, and you'd find somethin' to spend it on," Calhoun said. It was the closest he ever came to humor.

Aggie laughed. "Reckon I would at that." She sobered. "It's true, though, that it'd cause nothin' but trouble. Gold fever's been the ruin of more men and women than I could count."

"But, Aggie . . ." Helena protested.

"Hush, child," Aggie said fondly. "Good lookin' young thing like you won't have no trouble comin' up with gold when she needs it. That's ill-gotten money and would be the ruination of us all. Mister Calhoun's right—it should be brought back to Fortitude. It's those folks' money."

Fortitude was the same as Calhoun remembered it. Cochrane, the liveryman-mayor, was surprised as all get-out to see Calhoun, and said so.

"Told you I'd bring that money back soon's I took care of Dunleavy and his men," Calhoun said testily.

"Took you a spell, though," Cochrane said unapologetically. "We all figured you took the money and had hightailed it for God knows where."

"Took a little longer than I'd figured," Calhoun allowed.

"Had trouble findin' 'em?" Cochrane asked.

"Sort of," Calhoun said with a shrug.

"Pshaw," Aggie threw in. She explained about the happenings at Misfortune, how Calhoun had saved her and Helena, and had been wounded in the process.

"Sorry, Mister Calhoun," Cochrane said. "I didn't know."

Calhoun shrugged. He mounted his chestnut and rode to the cemetery. He found the stone with Mary's name chiseled on it.

"Did a fine job, didn't they?" the old mountain man, Charles Peckham, said quietly from behind Calhoun. "She'd be proud."

"I expect so," Calhoun said. He was as pleased as

he could be with the stone, considering what it was for. "I'm obliged."

Peckham shrugged. "Like I said, I owed ol' Barefoot."

"One more thing I'd like to ask of you, Mister Peckham." Calhoun paused. He never liked to ask favors of anyone, but this one had to be asked. "You're on good terms with the Utes?"

"Good as anyone's, I reckon. Why?"

"I'd be obliged if you was to find Mary's people. Tell 'em what happened."

Peckham half grinned. "I been lookin' for an excuse to ride thataway," he said. "I'll do it."

The two men shook hands and Calhoun rode back into town.

The two women had created quite a stir, as was to be expected, and both had men swarming around them like bees on new spring wildflowers. Still, Helena came over to him as soon as she saw him, and they spent that night together in the narrow, quilt-lined bed that Calhoun had shared with Mary not so long before.

As was usual, Calhoun was up early. He dressed quietly in the dark and gathered up his belongings. Then he bent and lightly kissed Helena on the cheek. With his saddle and saddlebags slung over his shoulders, he walked out. He saddled the chestnut horse, and then had a quick, filling breakfast at the restaurant.

Less than an hour later, Calhoun was riding

north out of Fortitude. He was aware of Aggie watching him from a window. He tipped his hat in her direction. She smiled at him. Then he was gone.

Clint Hawkins is the pseudonym of a newspaper editor and writer who lives in Phoenix, Arizona.

Saddle-up to these

THE REGULATOR *by Dale Colter*
Sam Slater, blood brother of the Apache
and a cunning bounty-hunter, is out to
collect the big price on the heads of the
murderous Pauley gang. He'll give them
a single choice: surrender and live, or go
for your sixgun.

THE REGULATOR—Diablo At Daybreak
by Dale Colter
The Governor wants the blood of the
Apache murderers who ravaged his
daughter. He gives Sam Slater a choice:
work for him, or face a noose. Now
Slater must hunt down the deadly rene-
gade Chacon…Slater's Apache brother.

THE JUDGE *by Hank Edwards*
Federal Judge Clay Torn is more than a
judge—sometimes he has to be the jury
and the executioner. Torn pits himself
against the most violent and ruthless
man in Kansas, a battle whose final ver-
dict will judge one man right…and one
man dead.

THE JUDGE—War Clouds
by Hank Edwards
Judge Clay Torn rides into Dakota where
the Cheyenne are painting for war and
the army is shining steel and loading
lead. If war breaks out, someone is
going to make a pile of money on a river
of blood.

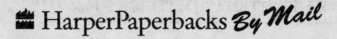